# THE FAMILY

S. E. GREEN

# ONE
# LEAH

*Present Day*

I MOVE AROUND THE KITCHEN, pouring myself another mug of coffee, retrieving a container of fresh mango from the refrigerator, and washing Walker's oatmeal bowl.

Situated in North Georgia's Appalachian Mountains, our log home overlooks the river that feeds a nearby lake. It's April when the water and the air temperatures often merge, blanketing the area in fog.

I worry about Walker's drive down the mountain to work. In the snow, visibility tends toward bright and crisp, but in the fog, he often relies on memory to navigate. He's been doing it successfully for years. Still, I worry.

On the corner of the honed granite kitchen island rests my iPhone, plugged in and charging. It chimes, indicating someone is at our front door. A glance at the clock shows it's 7:30. That's odd. We're remote and not expecting anyone or a delivery.

I bring up the security camera as the person knocks.

An image flickers onto the screen. Outside my front door is a very skinny girl with her head down, bony shoulders poking through a thin, long sleeve T-shirt. Her dull brown hair is shorn to a buzz cut. She turns, looking directly in the camera.

I gasp. *It can't be.*

My beautiful and curvy daughter is a skeleton, a shadow of her former self. Her once flush cheeks look pallid. Her vibrant and happy eyes sit dark and sunken in.

She knocks again. I trip over my own feet as I race from the kitchen, disengage the alarm, and fling open the front door. "Nyla? Oh my God. Nyla!"

"Hi," she hesitantly responds.

My daughter's voice melts through me. *She* melts through me. I haven't seen or heard from her in over five years.

My heart pounds. I don't know what to do. My gaze bounces past her to the driveway where my Mercedes sits, beyond that the trees, and the road further on. How did she get here? What's happened?

I look back at her.

Her mouth trembles into an unsure smile.

The gesture snaps me back. Tears burst free. I step onto the front porch and wrap my daughter in a strong embrace. I hug her hard, more than aware of her delicate frame, and not caring. Nyla doesn't return my hug. Instead, she folds her arms over her chest and tucks in beneath my chin. Just like she used to do as a child.

---

NOW WRAPPED IN A BLANKET, Nyla sits at the kitchen table, her feet up on the chair as she cradles her bent knees. I made her pancakes, her favorite, but she's barely taken one bite. Instead, she stares out at the river. I can't stop looking at her bony knees sticking through holes in her black leggings.

*When was the last time she ate?*

*Where has she been?*

*Does her father have anything to do with this?*

I want to ask all of those questions and more, but I won't risk saying the wrong thing.

Not again.

Instead, I clear my throat and ask what I hope is a neutral question. "You don't have any things?"

Nyla shakes her head.

"Do you need a doctor?"

"No."

"How did you get here?"

"I hitchhiked."

The thought of her hitchhiking makes my stomach hurt. "From where?"

"Tennessee."

"How did you know I'd be here at Grandma's place?"

"I didn't."

Her response confuses me. I moved here from Atlanta two years ago. If she didn't know I'd be here, what was she going to do—break in?

"You live here now?" she asks, still looking out at the river.

"Yes."

"No more 'big city'?"

"No."

"Oh."

Some odd seconds tick by.

"I'm so very happy to see you," I add, still in shock that she's here beside me. It's all I can do not to cry again.

Nyla finally looks over at me, giving a closed-lip smile that reminds me of her father. "Me too."

A shaky breath leaves me. I concentrate on not getting emotional. It's one of the things that always annoyed Nyla. But a tear escapes anyway. I press a knuckle to the corner of my eye, praying she doesn't see it.

"I'm going to bed now. Okay?" Nyla asks.

"Why don't you grab a hot shower and I'll get the room ready."

―――――

I PREPARE THE GUEST ROOM, stripping the bed and putting on clean sheets. In the connecting bathroom, I hear the running shower. She's been in there forever. At first, she left the door open, but I closed it to give her privacy.

When she first left our condo in Atlanta, I convinced myself it would only be a few weeks. Every mother and daughter had fights. Nyla would be back after she calmed down. In truth, I initially liked the calm that came with her absence.

But weeks turned to months.

Months to a year.

Then two, three, four...

I'd been angry, then bitter. Indifference came after that, followed by deep concern. At a minimum, why couldn't Nyla―or her father―return my messages?

Around the two-year mark, the phone numbers I had for them no longer worked. It left me with no choice. I settled into acceptance. Living with her father was what Nyla always wanted. Clearly, it was going well.

Except―from the look of her―it didn't.

The shower turns off. A moment goes by as I finish

prepping the guest room. The door opens. She emerges wearing a long black robe. It's the same robe I gave her for Christmas just before she turned eighteen.

Weeks later, she was gone.

Nyla looks around the room. Over in the corner sits an opened box of her clothes that I brought when I moved here from Atlanta.

"Does someone else live here with you?" she asks. "I saw men's boots at the door."

"Walker and I live together now. You met him once, back when we were dating. Do you remember?"

"Yeah, I remember."

"He'll be home later today. You can re-meet him then."

"Okay."

I pick up the pile of dirty sheets. Or more like stale. It's been months since I changed them. "Are you hungry? Thirsty?"

Nyla crawls onto the bed. "Just tired." She curls into a ball on top of the comforter. With her back to the door, she closes her eyes.

"The sheets are clean. You're welcome to get under the covers."

"I'm fine."

"Okay." Quietly, I take a step away. I fully intend on leaving and going downstairs, but I end up lingering in the doorway, simply watching her sleep.

It's like I'm afraid if I blink, she'll once again be gone.

# TWO
# NYLA

*Five Years Earlier*

CLOSING THE PASSENGER DOOR, Nyla went to stand beside Ava, a girl about her same age—eighteen or so. Ava had been the one to pick her up at the bus stop.

"Well, this is it," she said. "What do you think?"

Nyla breathed. "Serene."

A large run-down farmhouse sat in the middle of nowhere. Rural Middle Tennessee, actually, but to Nyla, it seemed nowhere.

Over to the right, a man dressed in jeans, a thick flannel jacket, and gloves chopped wood. Through the windows of the farmhouse, Nyla saw two women rushing around—cleaning, setting the table, and hurrying in and out of rooms double-checking things.

On the broken porch, another man replaced rotten wood with fresh planks.

The scent of fire filled the January frigid air.

In the side yard, a decrepit barn with no doors showed a

bundled-up teenage girl with a chalkboard giving an alphabet lesson to two toddlers wrapped in blankets. In the rear, a makeshift greenhouse offered a peek of a woman pruning and picking while simultaneously breastfeeding a newborn.

All around snow fell.

The sound of a distant engine came, hiccupping and in need of repair.

"That would be Paul," Ava said. "I can't believe he's your father. You're so lucky."

"I know." Nyla smiled. She'd waited forever for this moment.

Ava turned to her, frowning a bit. "Don't be upset he didn't pick you up. He had a lot to do today."

"I'm not upset."

Ava grinned. "Oh good." It struck Nyla how naturally pretty her new friend was. With deep dimples and creamy skin, giant brown eyes with thick lashes, and shiny blond hair that almost touched her butt, Ava could easily model for any number of clean beauty products. Even her long bohemian skirt matched her natural vibe.

An old blue truck peaked a hill, slowly making its way toward the farm. All around, hundreds of pines dusted in snow provided privacy from the outside world.

As the truck drew closer, Nyla recognized her father behind the wheel. She waved, feeling giddy. Sure they talked once a month and visited each other occasionally over the years, but this would be the first time Nyla and her father lived together since she was eight.

The truck ground to a stop beside the car. The driver's door creaked open. Dressed in work boots, corduroy pants, and an old leather jacket, her father emerged. He looked exactly like she remembered—average height and lean with coal-black thin hair he wore straight down his back. As usual, his face was clean shaven, not because he couldn't grow hair but because he thought it better defined his jaw not to have it. He'd told Nyla that one time and she always remembered.

Nyla dropped her duffel bag in the snow and ran to him. Laughing, he picked her up and swung her around.

"You're here," he said.

"I sure am."

He kissed her on the cheek before putting her on her feet.

Behind her, Ava approached. He turned his attention to the other girl. His eyes smiled as she came up beside him, carrying Nyla's duffel. He opened both arms, cradling a girl under each. He looked from Ava to Nyla and back. "You are officially in charge of my daughter. She deserves all the goodness in the world. Take good care of her."

"I will," Ava assured him.

He looked at Nyla. "Did she show you around? Have you met everyone?"

"Not yet," Ava quickly answered. "We just pulled in."

Nyla's dad began walking. "Well, let's remedy that." He squeezed Nyla. "You will love it here."

"I already do, Dad."

"It's not like any place you've ever lived."

---

NYLA MET everyone and remembered none of their names. She'd have Ava remind her later.

Between fresh fruit and vegetables from the green-house, wind and solar energy, and reclaimed water, the house and outbuildings made up a self-contained and supporting farm.

What Nyla first thought to be a run-down homestead proved to be a thriving and sustaining one.

"We share everything here." Ava walked Nyla in and out of neutral rooms with homemade pine furniture and peeling white baseboards. "Downstairs is our communal area where we eat, play games, music, or whatever. Upstairs is where we sleep."

They climbed the steps, a few creaking under their weight, and came to a landing. Two doorways on the right showed bedrooms, one with bunk beds and another with a queen bed—all done in the same neutral/white/pine as downstairs. Straight ahead sat an average bathroom. On the left, another room held racks and shelves filled with clothes and another a king bed.

Ava headed into the room with clothes. She placed Nyla's duffel along the wall. "This room is like a giant closet. As I said, we share everything, and that includes clothes. You'll put your things in here, but you're welcome to wear whatever."

"That sounds cool."

"It is." Ava grinned. She walked across the hall and into the room with bunk beds. Three bunks to be exact—one on the right, one on the left, and the last along the back wall—all done in matching crème quilts. She pointed to the right top one. "That one is yours."

"The last time I slept in a bunk bed was at summer camp in middle school." Nyla looked around. "No computers or TVs?"

"No, none of that," Ava said. "We do have a landline phone for emergencies. Did you bring a cell?"

"I did."

"You'll need to give it to Paul. He'll recycle it."

"Okay," Nyla answered without issue. While her friends had always been glued to their phones, she never cared. "Is my dad the leader?"

"The leader?" Ava laughed. "Leader of what?"

Nyla felt stupid. "Nothing."

"We don't have a 'leader.' We make decisions together."

Quickly, Nyla counted how many people she'd met. Including her, there were three teenage girls, three women, three men, two toddlers, and one baby. "Everyone lives here then?"

"Yes." Ava led the way out of the bunk room and into the bathroom.

A shelf above the claw-foot tub held bars of soap and various bottles of shampoo and conditioner—all homemade. Another shelf above the pedestal sink contained cups with wood toothbrushes. A variety of combs, shaving supplies, and feminine items lined the shelves of an open cabinet.

Ava said, "We share this bathroom. We also have an outhouse and a creek nearby. I tend to bathe in it, even in the winter."

Nyla always had her own bathroom. Her own bedroom. Her own things. She didn't know how to share.

Ava took her hand. "You're going to love it here. Just wait."

---

THEY NOW SAT around a long picnic table, sharing platters heavy with brown rice, lentils, steamed broccoli, sliced tomatoes, and giant rounds of pineapples. Nyla's father was directly across from her.

Laughter and conversation filled the air over lunch.

Did they do this for all three meals? Nyla liked it. Her father may not be the leader, but it certainly appeared that way. He drew the attention of all. He led the conversation. He pulled people in.

Eventually, lunch ended. On the wall of the eating room a large chalkboard assigned chores: greenhouse, food prep, house cleaning, outhouse, fire wood, laundry, kitchen, and various others.

Ava grabbed Nyla's plate. "I'm on clean up."

"What should I do?" Nyla asked.

"Come with me," her father answered.

Everyone else spread out, most resuming what they'd been doing when Nyla first arrived.

Beside the door, a row of hooks held multiple jackets. She found her red down one and slipped it on. Her father waited on the porch. She joined him there.

"Ava show you around?" Dad asked.

"She did. I like her."

"Me too."

"How old is she?"

"Sixteen."

That surprised Nyla. She thought Ava was her age.

Nyla glanced over at her father. "How long have you been living here, Dad?"

"A while." He inhaled a long breath and blew it out slowly like he savored the exhalation. "Any problems with Leah?"

"No. I left her a note."

"You tell her where you were going?"

"No."

Smiling, he offered his arm and Nyla stepped in. He smelled like wood and baked bread. "Do me a favor. Don't call me 'Dad.' Call me Paul."

"Oh..." Nyla frowned. "Why?"

"First names put everyone on the same plane. Titles of authority aren't needed."

She didn't realize "Dad" was a title of authority. But, if he wanted it, then, "Okay." It bummed her. She loved calling him Dad.

They continued standing, him breathing deeply.

"Do you own this farm?" Nyla asked.

"No, we all do."

She didn't know a lot about owning property, but that seemed odd. "You mean like you all went in on it together?"

"Technically, June owns it. She's generously gifted it to whoever we bring into our family."

"Which one is June?"

"She's got the newborn baby. She also mans the greenhouse."

Speaking of, June stepped through the front door clothed in a long thick sweater, fingerless gloves, and carrying the newborn in some complicated sling that wrapped around her body. She had small eyes and lips that didn't close over her giant teeth.

Dad—*Paul*—beckoned the woman over. Still holding onto Nyla, he caressed the baby's head with his free hand. "Nyla, this is Baby Sarah. Your sister."

# THREE
# LEAH

*Present Day*

THE AFTERNOON HOURS ROLL BY. I spend them checking on Nyla, looking at old photo albums, and re-reading cards she gave me over the years. On our roller coaster of a relationship, it's evident—based on my daughter's cards—when the two of us were up and when we were down. Sometimes she'd write a sweet sentence or two on the greeting card; other times she simply signed her name.

The last message, written on a sticky note and pressed to the microwave, read simply: I'M GOING TO LIVE WITH DAD. GOODBYE.

I divorced Paul when Nyla was eight. The legal process was contentious, expensive, and messy. I got full custody. Paul moved away. I didn't know where. He seemed to always be in a new state when he called—once a month—to talk to Nyla.

The begging started immediately.

*Please let me live with Daddy.*

*Please let me live with Daddy.*

*Please let me live with Daddy.*

It didn't help that Paul encouraged it. That he put thoughts in her head. *I want you to come live with me, but your mother won't allow it.*

That was one hundred percent true. There was something off with Paul. Always had been. Though to this day, I can't tell you what exactly.

*I hate you for not letting me live with Daddy!*

Yeah, raising Nyla had not been easy.

I'm about to put everything away when the garage door goes up. Walker's home.

I slide the cards back into the manila envelope, before closing it inside a photo album. The garage door goes back down. Walker comes in, treading the hall toward the kitchen where I sit at our round table topped in glass.

He steps through the archway. His eyes track over the items in front of me, the kitchen, out the windows toward the river, then back to me. "Where is she?" he asks.

"Sleeping. She's been that way all afternoon."

"Is she okay?" He comes over, kisses me, and sits beside me. He takes my hand. "Did she tell you anything?"

"Not really."

"Where's she been? Has she been with her father this whole time?"

"I don't know. She looks bad," I whisper, feeling the storm of emotion I tamped down earlier. "Really bad." Hot tears come, rushing free. I do nothing to stop them.

Walker hugs me. "It's okay. She's home now. That's what matters."

WALKER AND I MAKE DINNER. We eat. We linger in the living room. Nyla never shows. Eventually, we go to bed.

I don't sleep. Instead, I check on her nearly every hour, finding her in the same position—curled on her side with the black robe secured around her.

Come morning I make a big breakfast, hoping she shows. With everything on warm, I sit at the kitchen table, sipping strong coffee while Walker scrolls his phone.

What if Nyla sleeps all day today as well?

Is that even possible?

Eventually, she has to wake up.

As if my daughter reads my mind, Nyla shuffles hesitantly into the kitchen.

I straighten. "Good morning."

"Morning," she mumbles.

Walker looks up. I told him what to expect, but to see her upright is a different story.

She wears a deep blue tank top, white cotton shorts trimmed with lace, and long burgundy and silver striped socks that come up over her knees. Around her neck, she looped a pale pink fuzzy scarf that I recognize as my own.

Which means Nyla's been in our room.

Walker stands. "It's good to see you again." He smiles, walking toward her and extending a hand.

She shakes it. "Good to see you also." She motions to his auburn goatee and tortoiseshell glasses. "You look the same."

He pats his flat stomach. "A few extra pounds, but yes, the same." He nods over to the stove and oven where I left everything on warm. "Your mother made all sorts of things. I hope you're hungry."

"I am."

I motion to the place setting I'd prepared for her. "Why don't you sit here so you can look out the window and enjoy the view? There's no fog today, just the great morning sun and the sparkly water. I'll get you food. A little bit of everything sound good?"

Nyla nods.

While she makes herself comfortable, I pick up her plate and move around the kitchen island. I take my time with the presentation—placing a waffle center plate and drizzling it with warm raspberry sauce. I spoon some scrambled eggs to the side and add a few slices of crisp bacon.

I place it in front of her.

Her eyes widen. "That looks fabulous."

Laughing, I sit back down.

Using her bare hands, Nyla digs in. She devours the food, shoving so much into her mouth at a time that she can't close her lips. Loudly, she eats, pausing only to gulp water. Walker tries not to stare, but the effort proves difficult. I try as well, but the sight of my emaciated daughter pushing food into her mouth wrenches my heart. I want to tell her to slow down, that she's going to make herself sick, but I keep silent.

When she finishes, she lifts the plate and licks it clean. Then she does the same with each finger and thumb.

After that, she sits back, closes her eyes, and sighs.

"D-do you want more?" I ask.

"No, thank you." Nyla brings her feet up into the chair, cradling her bony knees with her equally bony arms. She opens her eyes. "That was delicious."

Walker and I exchange a stunned look.

Then, we laugh.

So does Nyla. She picks up the empty mug at her place setting. "I'll take coffee now."

Next to me sits the carafe. I hand it to her and she pours. "You still like condensed milk in it?" I ask.

"I think so." Nyla shrugs. "It's been forever. Let me have it and I'll let you know."

I do, Nyla tries it, and grins.

"Guess that's a yes." Walker pushes back from the table and takes his plate into the kitchen. "Nyla, I'll see you later. I'm off to work."

She looks over her shoulder at him. "What do you do?"

"I'm in IT."

Nyla looks at me. "You used to do IT stuff."

"I still do. Part time now. I mostly work from home." I go to Walker, giving him a quick kiss. "Was thinking steak tonight on the grill?"

"Perfect." With a wave to Nyla, he leaves.

I begin cleaning the kitchen. "What do you want to do today? I have a few hours of work, but that's it."

"You used to work a lot, Leah. I remember."

Something in the room shifts, going from the fun of just a few seconds ago to heavy. Nyla never called me Leah before. Not even at her angriest. Cautiously, I answer, "Yes."

"But not anymore."

"Not so much, no."

"How? Does Walker pay the bills?"

"Some, yes. Others I pay. Why?"

"Paul never paid bills, did he?"

I hesitate, feeling things about to spiral out of control. One wrong word and I'll be in a head-to-head battle with my daughter. Again. But I'm not going to lie. I've done enough of that over the years to save a relationship that ended horribly anyway.

At least I don't feel so singled out hearing her call her father by his name as well.

"Not really, no. Paul didn't contribute much." I barely breathe as I wait for Nyla to jump to her father's defense.

But...she doesn't.

Instead, Nyla stands. "Think I'll go sit in that pretty sunshine. Want to join?"

———

THE SUN SHINES BRIGHTLY. With a crispness to the morning air, we sit side by side on the back porch swing sharing a blanket.

"How did you and Walker meet?" Nyla asks. "I don't remember."

"Through work."

"How long have you been living together?"

"Four years."

"How old is he?"

"Same age as me."

"And that is?"

I give my daughter an amused look. "You don't remember how old your mother is?"

"Fifty-five?"

"Yes, fifty-five."

She's silent for a second, soaking in the yard, surrounding mountains, and slow river. "I always thought it was funny Grandma called this place her 'little cabin.'"

I chuckle. "It is a bit big for a 'little cabin.'"

"I always loved coming here."

"I remember."

"Too bad we didn't move here sooner."

"I really couldn't. Not with work."

"So, you would move here for Walker and not me?"

"I'm not sure I understand."

"It doesn't matter." She sighs. "It's just I always hated Atlanta." She glances over at me. "Is Walker okay with me being here?"

"Of course." I wait for the next question, but there isn't one. Instead, Nyla looks pensively back toward the river. I want to backtrack and get clarification. Why would she say that about moving here for Walker and not her?

Her father communicated like this—with passive-aggressive statements and questions.

Given that she left me to live with him, I shouldn't be surprised.

Shifting on the swing, I look at the side of her face. "Nyla, where is your father?"

She doesn't answer. Her body stills. She falls even more quiet. Seconds roll by. Just when I decide she's not going to respond, Nyla says, "I'm... not sure."

# FOUR
# NYLA

*Five Years Earlier*

NYLA COULDN'T REMEMBER a time when she didn't want to live with her father. She didn't hate her mother; they just didn't get along.

They'd never gotten along.

Clashing heads; didn't see eye-to-eye—whatever you wanted to call it. Nyla's grandmother said they were too similar.

Whatever.

Nyla *was not* similar to her mother.

Her mom spent too much money on frivolous things. She didn't recycle. She threw away food only a day old. She never stopped working. Her mother enrolled her in Atlanta's best private school. She made her take piano lessons. She hired a private tennis coach. She sent her to various pricey camps. She forced her into mother-daughter spa days.

Yet none of that made Nyla happy. She always wanted a simple life, secluded from society.

And now here she was.

It had been four months since she first arrived. Winter quickly became spring. She now knew everyone's names, and though they did share chores and general upkeep, everyone did have a main responsibility in the family.

Except for Nyla. She helped everywhere and succeeded at nothing. She overwatered the greenhouse. She made the kids cry. She burnt bread. She left streaks when cleaning. She bled on Paul's shirt while sewing a button. She slammed her thumb with a hammer. Despite the years of piano lessons, Nyla played like a six-year-old kid.

She blamed her mother. If she hadn't spoiled Nyla so much, she'd have practical skills to contribute.

Worst, she suspected her new family tolerated her only because of Paul.

———

ON A CHILLY APRIL EVENING, Nyla stood on the front porch watching the old brown car drive away into the night. Paul drove with June beside him. In the back sat the other couple in the house, Randolph and Beatrice.

Behind Nyla, the front door opened. Dressed in light-weight cargo pants and a tee, Mark stepped out. Nyla liked Mark. He was a big man, standing well over six feet and thick with muscles. Every morning he shaved his head but kept his beard on the full side. She often wondered what he'd look like with hair. Mark had a kind face.

"Hi." He smiled warmly.

"Hi, back." She nodded to the brown car's taillights

disappearing down the long dirt road. "Where are they going?"

"It's a secret," he teased

Nyla gave him a playfully skeptical look. "I thought we didn't keep secrets here."

He chuckled. It made the corners of his eyes crinkle. "They're going into town. There's a night time swap meet they sometimes buy and sell at."

"Sell what?"

"Stuff from around here. Plants that June grows. Some of the wood pieces I whittle. Baked goods from Beatrice. Randolph repurposes small appliances. Sometimes Ava goes to play her guitar and sing. And Karly's homemade clothes are always a hit."

Nyla didn't know for sure but she guessed Karly, the eldest, to be about seventy. Mark was right—she did make awesome clothes. "Is that how this place generates money then?"

"Yes."

Nyla went back to looking out through the night. A quiet few seconds beat by. "How did you come to live here?" she asked.

"June inherited this place when her parents passed. Karly was a longtime friend of the family, kind of like a second mother to June. Karly moved in to keep June company and help her out. About five years ago, they ran an ad looking for a roommate. Both Paul and I answered that ad. They decided to offer us each room and board in exchange for keeping the farm up and helping with bills."

"What about Beatrice and Randolph?"

"They were driving by in that old brown car. She was in labor. We're so far out that getting to a hospital wasn't doable. She had the baby upstairs in the tub. They were living in that car. Now they live here. That's been three years ago now."

"And Ava?" Nyla asked.

"Ava's been here a year. She lost her parents in a car accident. She's Karly's granddaughter."

Surprised, Nyla looked over at him. "I didn't know that."

"Yep. Ava already knew Carrie," Mark said, referring to the other teenage girl. "I'm not sure how much you know about her, but when she got pregnant, her parents kicked her out of the house. She was living on the streets when Ava asked us if she and Little Carrie, then a one-year-old, could live here too. We didn't hesitate in saying yes."

Carrie named her daughter after her, so everyone called her Little Carrie. Nyla liked that a lot.

Mark stepped to Nyla, tugging gently on her ear lobe. "And now there's you."

No one ever tugged her earlobe before. Up close like this, Mark overwhelmed her with his body heat, height, and strong physique.

Her cheeks flushed.

She suspected he saw it as well because he smiled a little as he leaned down, coming face to face with her. For one suspended second, Nyla didn't breathe. Was he going to kiss her? She should be disgusted at the thought, shouldn't she? Mark was old enough to be her father.

Yet she might like to kiss Mark.

He didn't though. Instead, he said, "You're supposed to be inside watching Baby Sarah."

"I know, it's just...she hates me."

"She's a baby. She doesn't hate you." He slid a warm and large hand around the back of her neck and steered her toward the front door.

In the living room, Karly mended clothes. Ava strummed her guitar. Fifteen-year-old Carrie read to the toddlers. Mark moved across the room to stoke the fire. Another couple of weeks and it wouldn't be chilly enough for a fire. What a shame. Nyla loved the flames, the warmth, and the smell.

In the corner on a blanket, Baby Sarah cried.

Karly cast a withering look in Nyla's direction.

With a sigh, she retrieved the baby. She changed the baby's diaper. She fed the baby. She burped the baby. Nothing worked. She didn't know why they gave her baby duty. It's not like she had one of her own. She didn't know what to do. She had never even babysat before.

Eventually, Carrie took Baby Sarah from Nyla and, of course, the baby immediately quieted.

Nyla hovered awkwardly in the corner, looking at everyone else even though they paid her no attention. She thought about her failure with the baby, cleaning, cooking, sewing, and everything else.

She needed to find her niche, soon.

---

A WEEK LATER, everyone scattered the living room listening to Ava play the guitar and sing. They each sipped homemade wine, produced from grapes grown in the greenhouse. Nyla lay on the hardwood floor with a pillow under her head. She noted Ava wore a wraparound jean skirt that was originally hers. It pleased her that beautiful, gorgeous Ava would like her things.

Nyla shifted on the floor, glancing across the downstairs into the dining room where Paul currently wrote on the chalkboard, changing the chore list. Nyla would be tending the compost pile. *Good*, she thought, *I can't screw that up.*

Paul put the chalk down and turned, looking straight at her. He studied her, long and hard, with a look of dissatisfaction. She sat up. He waved her over.

When she stood in front of him, he said, "Nyla, I've noticed you're trying, but I've also noticed you're struggling. How do you feel here?"

"I feel good."

"Are you happy you came?"

"I am."

"Do you feel as if you're fitting in?"

"I'm trying. I promise I am. It's just all so new to me."

"I want you to feel comfortable. I want this to be your home. You came here for a reason. You were not happy with your mother and her superficial life."

Nyla's heart beat heavily in her chest. Where was this conversation going?

"Do you feel as if I abandoned you after the divorce?"

"No, I don't. I know you left because it was hard living with that woman."

He gave a knowing nod. "I don't blame you for not trusting me though."

"Why do you think I don't trust you?" Nyla asked.

Paul sighed. He looked past her shoulder into the living room where everyone still gathered listening to Ava. "It's just a feeling I have."

"I do trust you."

"Are you sure?"

"Yes, very sure."

"Good." Paul looked back at her. "I have to say, I thought you'd have found your footing by now."

Embarrassment warmed her face. "I'm sorry." She tried to make a joke, "I'm pretty good at tennis."

Thankfully, he chuckled at the joke. "Not much good that does us here."

"I know..."

"It's not your fault. Everyone knows the entitled life you came from."

Did he tell everyone that?

"But as long as you feel safe and at home, that's what counts." He placed a comforting hand on her shoulder. "I need you to learn a skill though. I didn't realize how unprepared you are for this type of life. You can't just tend a compost pile. The babies can do that. If you're going to live here, you need to contribute more productively. I can't keep making excuses for you. I don't want to see you go."

He'd been making excuses for her?

Why would he say, *I don't want to see you go?* Had the others suggested it?

"Will you think about it?" he asked.

"I will," she quickly assured him. "I'll do better. I'll come up with something."

"That's wise." He let go of her shoulder. "And I'm happy you trust me. Because I might have a *suggestion* of how you can contribute if you're unable to come up with one."

# FIVE

# LEAH

*Present Day*

NYLA'S RESPONSE FELT ODD.

*I'm... not sure.*

Then again everything about my daughter now is odd.

I left her outside on the porch swing. I only had two meetings plus emails and a few things to wrap up on my current project. Through it all, I barely focused. I dissected our morning conversation forward, backward, and everywhere in between.

I don't know what's going on, and I don't want her to vanish again. All I can do is proceed carefully until I gain a better grip on this new version of my daughter.

After my work stuff, I check on her, finding her still on the swing, awake but just staring at the river. The afternoon hours tick by. I allow myself to check on her once per hour. I don't want to smother her. I ask if she is hungry. I ask if she's thirsty. I tell her to come inside any time she wants. But she stays outside all day.

Now it's getting to six and dark out. The last time I looked, she'd dozed off again. Walker will be home any moment. I prep the steaks for the grill and salad to accompany it.

The garage door goes up. A moment later Walker comes in.

He kisses me. "How were things today?"

"Strange. We sat on the back porch for a while. She said a few things that I've been obsessing about all day."

"Like?" He steals a cherry tomato from the salad bowl.

"It's not important. I think I'm putting way too much thought into it. She hasn't come inside though."

"Well, based on her breakfast show, she's going to want dinner."

I chuckle. "Hopefully, she'll use utensils this time."

Walker lifts the platter with the raw steaks. "These ready?"

"Yep, grill away."

He steals another cherry tomato before disappearing outside to the grill.

I finish dressing the salad, then begin setting the table. The back door opens. Walker steps inside.

"There is no way you're already done grill—" my voice dies when I see his shocked face. "What is it?"

He holds up both hands. "I'm not going back out there until you take care of things."

Frowning, I step out onto the rear porch. I look to the swing, finding only the blanket there. I walk the length of the house. It's dusk with dark just around the corner. Our exterior lights flick on. I turn a slow circle, my gaze rolling over the grassy terrain, the trees, the river—

I gasp.

There stands Nyla, the river coming to her knees,

naked. Straight across our elderly neighbors sit on their dock watching in disbelief.

I grab the blanket off the swing and race from the porch, across the backyard, and straight into the river. I collide with her, wrapping the blanket around her.

"What are you doing?" I yell.

She looks at me in confusion. "Enjoying the water."

"Nyla, you can't just do that. I have neighbors. Not to mention Walker just got home."

She looks over her shoulder back toward the house. "Did he see?"

"Of course he saw. It embarrassed him."

"Oh." She shrugs. "Sorry." Holding the blanket around her, she walks past her discarded clothes, across the yard, and back into the house.

I do the only thing I can, I give my neighbors an apologetic wave, pick up my daughter's things, and follow behind her.

As I do, I note wet marks on the inside of her bra.

———

LATER AT DINNER, Nyla picks at her steak and salad. Whatever enthusiasm for eating that she had at breakfast is gone.

She's been in our room again as evidenced by the oversized blue and yellow graphic T-shirt that she wears that belongs to me.

It's not that I mind if she wears my things; I would just like her to ask permission first.

Silently, she fiddles with the same bite of steak she's been fiddling with for the past ten minutes. Walker's silent as well. But at least he's eating, all while doing his best not to look at Nyla.

The air around the table constricts with tension.

Her fork clanks as she sets it down and stands. "I'm not hungry. I'm going to bed."

"I'm sorry I yelled."

"Whatever."

"It's just I wasn't expecting you to be doing that."

She straightens. "Doing what? I'm not ashamed to be naked. Not anymore."

I take a breath, promising myself I will be calm. "I didn't say you should be ashamed. There is a time and a place to be naked. In front of our elderly neighbors is not one of those times."

"Fine. I'm going to bed." She carries her plate to the counter, places a clean cloth over the uneaten food, and puts it inside the refrigerator.

She doesn't look at either one of us as she walks upstairs.

I turn to Walker. But now he's the one moving a piece of steak around the plate. I don't know what to say. I'm embarrassed. I'm confused. I'm upset.

"I'm sorry," I tell him.

"She's out of her element. Give her a few days to settle in."

It's not what I expected him to say. I adore this man. "I love you," I tell him.

He smiles. "I love you too."

We go back to our food. But I barely eat. It was getting dark out and everything did happen so quickly, but I did get a glimpse of my daughter's naked body. Plus, the wet marks on her bra.

Nyla has a baby.

# SIX
# NYLA

*Four Years Earlier*

FOR DAYS, Nyla's stomach ached. She wanted Paul to tell her his suggestion, but he didn't. It only served to ramp up her anxiety. Feverishly, she looked for a better way to fit in and contribute.

During this time, she became hyperaware of every word she spoke and every action she took. She didn't want anyone to think they'd be better off without her.

If she could just be more like Ava.

Everyone liked her. She possessed this potent power where anyone standing beside her seemed lesser, though Ava would never intentionally cause that. Nyla studied Ava's every move. She absorbed her every word. She soaked in her laughter. She followed her around the farm. Ava fascinated her. Not only with her great beauty and effortless style, but her pulsing energy. She electrified whatever room she entered. Nyla hated the plainness of her own face. Why wasn't she a great beauty? She hated the dull unoriginal clothing choices she made. She tried copying Ava's bohemian look but failed miserably.

"Why do you keep watching me?" Ava asked her one afternoon, annoyed.

"I'm sorry. Everyone likes you, and no one seems to like me. I'm trying to figure out how to be more like you."

"*That's* what's going on?" Ava sighed. "I think you're perfect. Just be yourself. Okay?"

"Okay," Nyla agreed, though she had no clue how to do that.

---

AT DINNER ONE SUMMER NIGHT, Ava suggested to June, "You should start growing healing herbs in the greenhouse. Nature gives us what we need, right?"

June brightened. "You read my mind. I've been researching. I can't believe I haven't already begun doing so." She retrieved a tattered hard cover book from the kitchen and brought it back to the table.

Nyla stared at the title: *The Good and Bad Side of Herbs.*

Paul sat in his usual spot beside June. He leaned in to look at the book, but instead of doing that, he stared at Ava's face. She didn't notice. Her attention stayed fixed on June.

But Nyla noticed.

She looked back to the book, zeroing in on the words *Bad Side.* She looked around the table. No one paid her attention. Not even Mark.

It was at this exact moment that Karly suffered a stroke —right there at the dinner table among conversation, laughter, and Paul staring at Ava.

Though Nyla didn't know it at the time, this would also be the second she suddenly held a role.

Nyla became Karly's caregiver.

Paul never did make his...suggestion.

---

SUMMER MOVED INTO FALL. Nyla spent every day and night tending to Karly. Nyla bathed her. She fed her. She read to her. She exercised her. She ran up and down the steps getting things Karly needed.

If you would've asked Nyla what she wanted to do one day, caregiving would have been the absolute last thing she would have picked.

But there she was on a November evening dabbing soup from the corner of Karly's mouth when Ava walked in and sat on the floor next to her grandmother's bed. Nyla finished cleaning Karly's mouth and stepped away.

"Thank you for taking care of my grandmother," her friend quietly spoke. "All this time and I've never told you that."

Her voice filled Nyla with something extraordinary and warm. "You're welcome."

From under Karly's bed, Ava pulled out a basket and continued knitting a sweater she'd been working on a few days now. "Want to sit?" her friend asked.

Yes, Nyla very much wanted that. "Mark told me about your parents," she said, realizing how much time had gone by since he told her. She should've said something sooner to Ava. "How old were you when it happened?"

"Fifteen."

"I'm so sorry."

"Thank you."

Ava smiled a little. They fell into silence after that. Ava's nimble fingers worked.

"You're good at that," Nyla told her sometime later.

"I can teach you if you want."

"Really?"

"Sure."

Ava showed her how to do a single crochet stitch. It surprised Nyla how quickly she picked it up. See, she only needed someone to have a little patience with her.

---

WINTER CAME. Nyla turned nineteen. She'd officially been living with her new family for one year. The past six months of which she dutifully, *resentfully* cared for Karly.

The older woman required so much that Nyla rarely interacted with anyone else. She stopped going down for meals. She stopped going to the common room for music or games. She stopped going outside. She simply stopped existing really.

She wished Karly would die.

But then what? Nyla would be back to not contributing in some significant way. Sure, she knew how to do a single crochet stitch but nothing else.

No, Nyla needed the old lady to live.

The thing though about hiding away in a room? Others forgot you existed. They talked openly.

Like when Paul and June argued outside in the hall. Or rather June argued as Paul remained stoic. *I've seen you watching Ava*, June spat. *Paranoia leads to distrust*, Paul calmly replied. *Distrust links back to paranoia. What a vicious, vicious cycle you're in.*

June wasn't wrong. Paul did watch Ava a lot. He

watched her comb her hair, wash her face, clean the house, and once he "accidentally" walked in on Ava while she changed clothes.

Did this bother Nyla? Of course, but it didn't seem to bother Ava, so Nyla let it go.

For the time being.

Yes, Nyla's new family talked openly, but they also engaged in sex.

Nyla didn't want to judge, but Beatrice had been cheating on Randolph for months now. It always occurred in the day when everyone did chores. Mark and Beatrice sexed it up in the bathroom, in her and Randolph's room, and even on Paul and June's bed.

From her spot on the top bunk, Nyla had a clear shot across the hall into Paul and June's room where she witnessed the whole thing. Whatever passing interest she may have once held in Mark sufficiently died when his bare butt pounded into Beatrice.

---

WINTER MOVED INTO SPRING.

When Nyla first arrived, she'd been enthusiastic and overwhelmed with the community, the atmosphere, and the collective thinking. The shift that happened came slightly. No longer did they make decisions as a group.

Paul took over as the leader.

It did not oppress the house. On the contrary, it thrived. Ava created new music and knitted everyone warm scarves. Carrie eagerly tended to the kids. June talked animatedly about a rare poison garden she put in. Mark built the children a swing set. Randolph devised a new irrigation system for the greenhouse. Beatrice flitted and floated around the kitchen, trying new recipes.

They all appeared so...happy.

Except for Paul.

Sure, he'd walk around and check out everyone's tasks, pretending interest. But often he stood alone brooding. Sometimes at night when Nyla lay awake, listening to the house sleep, Paul's door would open. He'd walk across the hall straight to the bunk room.

Sometimes he'd stand in the doorway, looking at everyone. Other times he'd walk over to Ava's top bunk. He even touched her hair once. Nyla barely breathed.

Then one year and four months to the mark of her arrival, Nyla woke up and climbed down the ladder to the floor.

The sun hadn't risen yet. She padded into the bathroom. Even on their vegan diet, she'd gained weight over the months of inactivity in being Karly's caregiver.

After doing her business, she walked back into the bunk room to find Paul leaning over Karly. Having heard Nyla walk in, he straightened up and turned. He held a pillow in his hands, and calmly, he placed it at the foot of the bed.

Though Nyla didn't want to admit it, she knew Paul had just ended Karly's life.

# SEVEN

# LEAH

*Present Day*

THE NEXT MORNING, Walker's already gone to work when Nyla steps into the kitchen. Today she wears her own clothes—a black tee and gray sweats that smother her skinny body. Around her neck, she's tied a pink kerchief.

"Good morning," she says, her tone timid.

I was braced for a battle, a moody daughter, the silent treatment, or whatever else. But not this. Nyla used to be many things, but around me? Never timid.

"Did you sleep okay?" I ask.

"Alright, I guess." She slides onto an island stool. "Are we okay?"

"Yes, we're okay." I smile. "I didn't do a big breakfast this morning. But there are loads of other things—oatmeal, cereal, eggs, protein bars, smoothies, etcetera. What are you in the mood for?"

Nyla slides back off the stool and retrieves her leftover dinner from the refrigerator. She doesn't warm it up. She simply selects a fork and knife, resumes her seat, and begins eating cold steak and wilted salad.

"You don't need to eat that."

"I want to," she says.

I watch her for a few seconds, unconvinced. But she seems content. I'm just happy to see her eat, this time with utensils. I pour her coffee and top off mine.

After a bite or two, she asks, "Do you think you'll ever marry Walker?"

"No, it's not what we want."

"How does that work though?"

"What do you mean?"

She sips her coffee. "Well, like what if he was in the hospital? You're not allowed to see him unless you're his wife, right?"

"No, that's outdated. We're each other's emergency contact. We're allowed to make medical decisions should that ever be an issue."

"He doesn't have children who would do that?"

"No, he never had kids."

She thinks about that, eating a few bites of flimsy lettuce. "What do you call him? Your companion? Your lover? Your boyfriend?"

Her questions come across as honest and curious. I don't detect the passive-aggressive tone from yesterday. "You mean like if I'm introducing him?"

Nyla nods.

"I say this is Walker, my partner."

"Oh." She moves back to the cold steak, cutting a couple of pieces before eating them. "That makes sense, I guess."

I finish my coffee and place the mug in the dishwasher. "Do you need or want a new cell? Yours was disconnected a long time ago."

She looks at me curiously. "Did you try calling?"

"Of course. I tried calling both you and Paul. Eventually, the lines went dead."

"I didn't know. I'm sorry."

Her apology comes through earnest, not flippant. "Thank you for saying that."

"You're welcome. To your question, no, I don't want, or need, a phone." She nods to the salad. "This lettuce isn't very good."

I laugh. She does as well.

"Do you want to do anything today? There's a cute town about ten miles from here with fun little shops. We could browse a bit and maybe grab a latte."

"Um..." She opts not to finish the salad and moves back to the two remaining bites of steak. "You don't have to work?"

"Yes, but only a couple of hours."

"I'd like to stay here if you don't mind."

"I don't mind a bit." I smile once more, letting her know it's truly okay. "I'm going to go anyway for errands."

As I'm leaving the kitchen, she says, "I'm curious. Do you and Walker always sleep spooned together?"

My feet stop moving. For a second, I'm not sure I heard her correctly.

Slowly, I turn. She's looking at me through alert and inquisitive eyes.

"Do you?" she repeats.

"How do you know we sleep spooned together?"

"Because I came into your room last night and watched you."

"What do you mean you watched us?" I barely get the question out.

"My head was hurting. I couldn't find medicine. I

came into your room to wake you. But I ended up not. You two were so intertwined and peaceful. I couldn't stop staring."

Her response seems so innocent and honest that I push the uncomfortableness away. "Next time wake me up, okay?"

"Okay." Finished with her food, she washes her plate, puts it in the drainer, and walks over to the window to look out over the river. She points. "Grandma used to own that land. Did you inherit it with this house?"

"I did."

"There used to be a really great trail through those woods. Is there still?"

"Yes."

She turns to look at me. "Can I go?"

"Of course. You don't need to ask for permission."

Her face flushes. "Sorry."

"Don't apologize." I turn away. "Take a jacket. It's nippy out."

The back door opens, then closes. I move to the kitchen window, watching her walk across the backyard. At the trail's entrance, she stops and turns. Carefully, she surveys this house, the surrounding trees, the river, the small dock, and the house across the river where the elderly couple lives.

There's something odd about the way she's scrutinizing the area. It's like she's memorizing the details. Or reaffirming what she already knew.

Or...looking for someone.

THAT NIGHT AFTER DINNER, Walker disappears upstairs to take a shower. I retrieve my bags from today's shopping trip. In the kitchen, Nyla is busy cleaning up.

"I bought you something today." On the kitchen island, I place a package wrapped in light yellow paper.

With her hands in soapy water, she pauses. Her surprised gaze goes from the package to me, back to the package. She says nothing.

"Open it," I encourage.

Hesitantly, she wipes her hands.

"I do own a dishwasher," I joke.

"Dishwashers are a waste of electricity and water," she mumbles like she's reciting someone else's words.

I ignore her. "Open it." I push the package her way.

Slowly, her eyes light up. I grin. Her fingers are careful as they pull at the ribbon and tape to reveal a white box underneath. She takes the lid off the box. Inside is a delicately folded green dress that ties in the front.

"For me?"

"Of course, it's for you."

Her jaw drops.

My God, I don't think she's had anything new since she left.

She picks it up, holding it out and staring at it in disbelief. "Thank you."

"You're welcome. Try it on."

"Now?"

"Yes, now."

Nyla begins to undress in the kitchen. I stop her. "How about the downstairs bathroom? In case Walker comes down."

"Oh, okay." She takes the dress into the bathroom. Again, she begins to undress. I pull the door closed.

I don't care if she undresses in front of me, but I do care about Walker. This new uninhibited Nyla takes me off guard. She used to scream at me if I accidentally opened a closed door and saw her in any stage of undress.

While she does her thing, I finish up in the kitchen—drying the skillet, washing the last plate, and putting things away.

She's been in the bathroom a lot longer than needed.

I prep tomorrow morning's coffee. I walk around downstairs, turning off the lights. Eventually, I go to the bathroom door. "Nyla?"

It inches open. She stands clothed in her gift, her face unreadable.

"What's wrong?" I look at the dress. "It's a bit big, but you'll gain weight."

"Why did you buy me this?"

Her question startles me. "Because I saw it and thought you'd look cute in it. Because I love you. You were a teenager the last time I bought you clothes. Plus, doesn't it feel good to wear something fun and new?"

"How much did this cost?"

"It doesn't matter. It's a gift."

"It does matter. I have plenty of clothes upstairs."

"I know that. But I've also noticed you've been digging around in my stuff."

"Is that a problem?"

"No." I sigh.

We stare at each other, her in the bathroom and me in the hall. A lot of odd seconds go by. Upstairs, I hear Walker moving around.

I don't know what to say. I turn away. "Listen, if you don't want it, I'll return it. No big deal. You're reading too much into the gesture. I'm going to bed. Good night."

At the top of the stairs, I don't look back at her. I simply walk into the master suite and close the door. Walker's climbing into bed.

"Did she like her gift?" he asks.

I don't reply.

He notices the shift in my demeanor. "What's wrong?"

"Nothing." I move into the bathroom and close the door. I stand at the sink and stare into the mirror. A frustrated woman stares back.

I had a daughter once. She was hardheaded, opinionated, and obstinate. She was also funny, sweet, and so very smart.

I don't know who that girl is downstairs. But that is not my daughter.

# EIGHT

# NYLA

*Four Years Earlier*

THE FAMILY BUILT a pyre in the side yard. Those who wanted to spoke a few words, then together they silently watched Karly's body turn to ash.

After, Ava gathered a mason jar full of her grandmother's ashes and disappeared into the surrounding trees. No one followed her. Paul insisted they give her space. Hours later she returned with an empty mason jar.

Not many days later, Nyla came across Ava dressed in a thick green robe, walking away from the house toward the creek to bathe.

Nyla ran to catch up. "Ava?"

Her long blonde hair moved with her as she turned around. Nyla hadn't cut her hair since arriving there at the farm. It grew long, but also straggly. She wished it held the thick luster of Ava's.

Nyla took her hand, giving it a gentle squeeze. "How are you?"

"I'm okay, I guess." Ava tried to smile, but her usual brilliance dulled. "Just sad. Karly was my only family."

Nyla noticed the chill in Ava's hand. She took it between both of hers and breathed on it. As she did that, she realized it might be an odd gesture. Nyla released it and took a step back.

But all seemed fine with Ava. She even asked, "Want to join me for a little dip?"

In the time Nyla lived there, she took her daily bath in the tub, inside, with the door closed. All year round, Ava used the creek.

Nyla said, "That water has to be freezing."

Ava retook her hand. "It's good for you. Come on."

They held hands across the yard, through the woods, and down to the water.

Ava had brought a towel along with the robe she wore. She handed it to Nyla. "You can use the towel." From the robe's deep pockets, she retrieved a bar of soap and broke it in half. Around her wrist, she wore several thick hair bands. She took two off, giving one to Nyla.

After securing her hair into a high bun, Ava slid from the robe and stepped naked into the water. The surface sparkled with the morning spring sunshine. Nyla tried not to stare at Ava's flawless body.

Carefully, Ava moved across the pebbles visible beneath the surface. The water grew deeper as she did. She paused when the water met her knees to place both halves of the soap on a rock that jutted from the surface. She moved forward, the water eventually coming up to her chin. "Wooh." She shivered, then giggled.

Nyla laughed.

She tied her thin hair up, gathered her courage, and quickly stripped. She'd never been a slender girl, tending toward self-consciousness about her weight instead of being out there and embracing it. Add to that the extra pounds from being Karly's caregiver and Nyla's body image went to the crapper.

But Ava brought something out in her.

Nyla stepped into the water. "Oh my God!"

They laughed.

She followed Ava's path across the pebbles until the water came to her chin as well. Her body flashed cold, then surprisingly hot. Probably because she just killed her nerve endings.

But it exhilarated her.

For a minute or so they swam around in the deep end. Then Ava retraced her steps until the water came to her knees. She worked the soap between her fingertips, getting good suds. She cleaned her body. Nyla wanted to stay ducked down in the water, watching Ava, but that crossed a creepy level she would regret.

No, instead she came to stand beside her friend and washed her body as well.

"You're not cold anymore, right?" Ava asked.

"Not really, no."

"My grandmother told me it's because your heart beats faster to warm your body. Also, the cold closes your pores so it traps the warmth in." She shrugged. "I don't know if all of that is true or not."

"Sounds plausible. I'd say google it, but we don't have internet."

"Do you think we're a commune?" Ava asked next.

The question—and change of topic—made Nyla hesitate. Yes. No. Yes? "Huh, I don't know."

"How do we make money now? No one has gone to the swap meet in forever. No one has gone anywhere except for

Paul to replenish our grains and beans. We all just exist here on this farm." Ava put her soap down and moved back into the deeper water. "I mean I know we're self-sustaining, but there are still bills. Like the mortgage and property taxes and the food Paul buys."

Nyla followed her. Somehow, she imagined her friend would know the answers to these questions. But they both appeared to be just as much in the dark.

Ava swam a circle, searching the woods around them, before coming back to look at Nyla. She lowered her voice. "I know my grandmother had money. What happened to it? Is that what everyone is living off of?"

"I don't know." Nyla's heart beat irregularly at their secretive tone. "Doesn't June have money? I mean, she owns the place, right?"

Ava looked again toward the woods. "'Paul sat down with me and June and worked it all out.' That's what my grandmother told me before her stroke."

"What did she mean by that?"

"I don't know," Ava whispered. "It's not just about the money. It's about Paul and how he thinks. You've missed a lot over the months you tended to Karly. I know he's your father. I don't want you to think I'm talking behind his back."

But isn't she? "It's okay. What did he say?"

"Just stuff like we have too much. Don't take it for granted. Think about what we eat. Remember giving is good for the soul. It makes you free."

Nyla frowned. "I don't think we have too much. My mother, now *she* has too much."

Ava laughed.

Together they swam to the shallow part and stood up.

A deep clearing throat resonated through the air. Nyla

whipped around, seeing Paul standing at the tree line, his feet braced wide, his arms folded, staring at Nyla, not Ava, Nyla.

She crossed her arms over her breasts. Her eyes widened. She stared in alarm at her father.

"You've put on weight," he said.

Embarrassment flushed her body. She wanted to cover herself, badly.

"Effective today, you will begin eating half portions at each meal."

"O-okay." Nyla nodded hard.

He looked from Nyla to Ava, who did not cover herself. She stood with her arms at her side, not defiantly, or even boldly, just comfortably.

Paul's gaze panned slowly down her. It reminded Nyla of that time he stared at Ava during dinner. Except now his eyes held something dark and curious that made Nyla uncomfortable.

"I heard you two talking."

Neither of them responded.

"If you want to know something, you need only ask. It's not smart or kind to have sneaky conversations." He kept staring at Ava like he wanted her to reply, but she didn't. Eventually, he continued, "No, we do not go to the swap meet anymore. We don't need to. Karly asked me to put her money toward what we needed around here. Giving is good for the soul. Perhaps you two need to think hard about that. Are you giving enough?" He looked at Nyla, then back to Ava. His eyes narrowed. "Because *both* of you can always do more."

ONE WEEK LATER, Paul and Ava kissed.

Nyla came from the house carrying laundry to be hung on the line. She rounded the corner and nearly dropped the basket of wet clothes.

In the open barn, Paul and Ava embraced in what appeared to be a consensual kiss.

Dread passed through Nyla, followed by an agonizing longing that she didn't understand.

Paul shifted, tilting his head. Ava stepped closer, pressing her body to his. He ran a hand along her side and around her back, holding her tight.

Nyla's stomach turned. The sight physically repelled her. She put a hand on her throat, quelling nausea.

She needed to tell someone. Now.

She spotted June in the greenhouse, oblivious. Carrying the basket, Nyla rushed across the side yard. As she passed the barn, Paul and Ava didn't see her. They stepped into a shadow to do God knew what. Nyla's heart pumped harder. Her pace quickened.

She burst into the greenhouse. "Paul's in the barn kissing Ava."

Hunched over her most recent batch of medicinal herbs, June jolted slightly. She looked at Nyla. She looked through the foggy plastic walls over to the barn, then back. She didn't move. Nyla's voice paralyzed her.

A muscle twitched in Nyla's face. She waited for June's response.

Yet, none came. Somehow, she remained calm.

Then, she broke.

June's eyes filled quickly with tears. They shocked Nyla. A beat of silence went by. She wished she could take the words back. Why did she tell June that?

But it was just wrong on so many levels. Paul had June and Baby Sarah. Paul was kissing a seventeen-year-old girl.

Paul was kissing Ava!

The news killed June. She covered her face. She cried, hard. She cried so hard that Nyla did as well.

"I'm sorry," Nyla muttered.

June pushed past her. She rushed from the greenhouse, running away from the property and into the trees.

Nyla stayed rooted in her spot, regretting her words. What did they accomplish? Nothing. Did she think June would confront Paul? Of course not. No one confronted Paul. No, Nyla's words pierced June.

The following morning, Nyla awoke to find June gone.

She left Baby Sarah behind.

---

IT SEEMED as if Nyla was the only one concerned that June left, yes, but more importantly without Sarah.

Given Nyla's track record with children, no one even suggested she take on the responsibility. She assumed that would fall to Carrie. It shocked Nyla when Ava walked up to her, smiling, with Sarah in one of those body carrier things.

"We're going for a walk. Want to join?"

Nyla didn't hesitate in saying yes. She would do anything if it meant spending time with Ava. Together they stepped out into a gorgeous and sunny day in May. Smiling sweetly, Ava clasped Sarah's hands and playfully jostled her.

Not too long ago they'd been sharing secrets in the creek. Ava seemed different now. Older. Mature.

Together Ava and Nyla strolled into the trees, heading

away from the creek where an unkempt trail wound through the pines.

Nyla blurted, "I saw you kissing Paul."

Ava pressed her lips together. Her cheeks pinkened.

"He's old enough to be your father."

She nodded.

"Did you want him to kiss you?"

"I don't know. It happened so quickly. It was my first kiss." She glanced over at Nyla. "Do you think that's why June left?"

"Yes, of course."

"Paul told me they weren't doing well. He confided in me about their troubles. It's probably best, I guess. Get rid of the toxic energy."

Toxic energy? That sounded like something Paul would say. "What about this property? June owns it."

"Paul's handling all of that."

Nyla's misgivings hardened into something real. What did that mean?

Ava pressed a kiss to Sarah's head. "Look how happy she is. I always wanted to be a mom."

"You're not her mom."

Ava's face fell. "I know that."

Nyla couldn't wrap her brain around this—Paul, June, Ava.

"I know this must be confusing. But June leaving was not bad. It was good. Meant to be even. We're a family here. Our paths wouldn't have crossed if all of this wasn't supposed to happen. We share a love for a different way of life, a love for each other. Paul says most people are too weak to love. Well, *I* love you. It's important to tell people that. I know you think Paul kissing me was bad, but it wasn't. You have to trust me. Do you trust me?"

*I love you.*

Did she just say that?

"Do you?" Ava asked.

Absently, Nyla nodded. *I love you* cycled her brain.

Ava began singing. Nyla heard her many times before, but something felt different now with the two of them alone in the woods. Like Ava sang only for Nyla, and no one else. Her voice floated through the trees, haunting, intense, and beautiful. It mesmerized Nyla. She listened, entranced.

*My love*
*There's only you in my life*
*The only thing that's right*

Nyla recognized the Lionel Richie song, and she loved it. She soaked in every word, meant solely for her. Her mind swam with what that might imply.

How did the two of them appear, she wondered—the talented gorgeous Ava singing a love song to the mundane inept Nyla?

Truth, she didn't care how they appeared. At this moment, clarity burned bright. She loved Ava and no matter what Nyla's misgivings may be, she would stay on this farm as long as Ava did.

# NINE
## LEAH

*Present Day*

THE NEXT MORNING, I awake to find Walker gone from his side of the bed. This is the day he works from home. I assume he's already downstairs in the office.

Nyla's bedroom door sits open, showing an empty and unmade bed. I don't hesitate. I walk straight in and around the room. I don't know what I'm looking for. She arrived with nothing. Still, I openly snoop, checking the bathroom, the closet, and the dresser drawers.

Under the bed, I find the dress I bought her wadded up and discarded.

My eyes narrow. My blood pressure rises. The tag is still attached. I shake it out and hang it on the bedroom door. I want her to know I've been in here. It's juvenile of me, but I don't care.

I start to make her bed and end up balling everything up and leaving it in the center of her mattress. She's a grown woman. She can make her own damn bed.

I'm now the one being passive-aggressive.

As I take the steps down, I hear Walker and Nyla in the kitchen.

"How long have you been up?" Walker asks. "I can't believe you cleaned all the grout in here."

"I wanted to contribute. It's important to do so."

"That's nice, but you're a guest."

"I thought I was family," Nyla teases.

"Yes." He laughs. "Of course."

"You want more coffee?"

"Sure."

I listen to Nyla move around the kitchen. I should take the last few steps and reveal myself, but I don't. I want to eavesdrop.

"What are you two ladies doing today?" he asks.

"I don't know about Leah, but I plan on walking the road in front of the house."

"Why?"

"Just because."

"Oh, well be careful. We don't get a ton of traffic up and down this mountain, but with the switchbacks and no shoulder, vehicles may not see you."

"I'll be careful. You hungry?" she asks. "I used to make an excellent omelet."

"Sure, sounds great."

That's true. Nyla did make a good omelet.

Walker sighs heavily and deeply. "Just look at that pretty day out there."

"Indeed."

I listen to Nyla crack eggs into a bowl.

He asks, "How are things going with your mom? I mean, overall."

"Fine, I guess."

"Is it strange to see her again after all these years?"

"Yeah, a little."

"I know you two had a rocky relationship, but you're both different now. Give it a chance."

Nyla is silent as she opens the refrigerator. Then she begins chopping vegetables. "Leah told me you don't have kids. Did you want them?"

"Sure, but it didn't work out for me."

"You still could. Find someone younger."

A confused chuckle leaves Walker.

"I'm sorry. I shouldn't have said that."

"That's... that's okay."

The skillet sizzles with butter. "What about Leah do you like, or love, I guess?"

"I *love* Leah. She's kind and intelligent. She's loving and funny. She's beautiful. I'll also tell you she's relieved you're back. You had her worried."

"Worried? Really? I thought she'd be happy that I left."

"Of course not. Listen, sometimes families do not get along."

"Ain't that the truth," she mumbles.

"I assume you've been with your father this whole time? In five years, I'm sure you had a squabble or two."

Nyla doesn't respond.

Time stretches. The omelet cooks. She gets a plate from the cabinet and serves them both. Walker tells her how delicious it is. She thanks him, then quietly she says, "Paul wasn't to be squabbled with."

There's something in her tone that I recognize—pain, confusion, fear—that has me quietly going back up the steps and into her room.

I put the dress where I found it and I make her bed.

My daughter ran from Paul and landed here on my

front door. Granted, she didn't know that I live here now, but I don't want to give her any cause to run back.

I want her to know she's safe.

---

I WON'T GO SO FAR as to say the day went fabulous, but it seemed somewhat normal.

Whatever normal means now.

Walker worked from home, as did I. Nyla busied herself reading, walking around outdoors, and she watched a little TV. She made us dinner—roasted chicken with wild rice and sautéed zucchini. More than once she commented how great it was to eat meat again. I took the comment in, wondering. Had she not eaten meat with her father? Was he a vegan now? Could they not afford it? I was curious, but I didn't ask follow-up questions.

I didn't want to jinx what fragile calmness we'd had throughout the day.

Conversation at dinner centered around uncomplicated things like the weather, food, and TV shows. The more we talked, the clearer it became she hadn't watched television in years. Again, I wondered. Did Paul not allow it? Could they not afford that as well?

We all went to bed early.

And now here I am next to Walker, typing Paul's name into a search engine. Where has he been this whole time?

I get back next to nothing. Paul has no social media. His last known address was the condo we shared in Atlanta.

"I thought things went well today," Walker says.

I put my phone down on the side table. I look at him, taking a few seconds to admire the planes of his handsome face. We aren't a love-at-first-sight story. We were friends first, then grew from there. I admire, and trust him, so very much. It's comforting. I never once admired or trusted Paul.

I trace a finger down his familiar cheek. "I love you so very much. I'm glad you came into my life."

"Ditto." He moves closer. We kiss.

"I must admit, I eavesdropped on your conversation this morning with my daughter."

"Oh?" He moves closer yet, nuzzling my neck.

"Thank you for the things you said about me."

"You're welcome," he murmurs.

Smiling, I slide down onto my back. He shifts on top of me. We get lost in one another's warmth and love. Sometimes when we're intimate it's fast and gets the job done. Other times it's slow and melting. Yet other times it comes in waves, stretching for what feels like an eternity as we explore each other's bodies.

Tonight, it's the eternity one where we take turns pleasuring one another in all kinds of delicious ways. Time melts away, leaving us cocooned in a world all our own. When he finally does enter me, it starts all over again— another wave—as we move into various positions, some meant for my pleasure, others for his, and yet others we both love.

After and beautifully spent, we lay beside one another, breathing and sweaty, our fingers linked. A small nightlight in the corner provides the only illumination in the master suite.

His fingers squeeze mine. "We don't do that version very often. But when we do, I am sufficiently satiated for however long it is before the next time."

"Well, maybe we need to do that version more often then."

"You won't get a complaint out of me." He squeezes my

fingers again before sitting up. Chuckling, he shows me his bedside clock. We both laugh. "That's a record. Three hours of lovemaking? Thank God we went to bed early." Naked, he stands up. "I need water, big time. You?"

"Yes, please." Smiling, I watch him walk over to the corner chair where we both draped our robes. He slides into his and turns.

He freezes.

"What's wrong?" I sit up.

He doesn't say a word. I'm not sure he could speak even if he wanted to. He points to the floor at the foot of our bed. I crawl forward, peeking over the footboard to see Nyla curled up on top of her comforter, sleeping.

"Nyla!" I shout, simultaneously wrapping the sheets around my naked body.

She startles awake.

"What are you doing?" I gasp.

My daughter sits up, looking first at me, then at Walker, then back to me. "Sleeping."

I scramble to turn on the bedside light. I'm at a loss. I look at Walker. His shocked eyes lock on mine. I'm sure he's thinking the same thing as me—What the...?

"You can't just come in here. How long have you been down there?"

Nyla shrugs. "I don't know. A while." She looks between us with this candid confusion that robs me of any more words. She honestly doesn't realize this is wrong. So very wrong on so many levels. I'm mortified.

Dressed in yet another one of my oversized tees, she stands up. "I'm sorry," she quietly says in a humiliated voice that tugs at me. She picks up the comforter. "I'll go." She moves toward the door, her head low, her feet shuffling in shame.

# TEN

# NYLA

*Four Years Earlier*

SPRING TRANSITIONED TO SUMMER. With June gone, things shifted. Carrie still cared for the children during the day, managing their activities and schooling. Thanks to June's detailed journal on the greenhouse, Nyla took over there, surprisingly not screwing things up. Paul managed daily routines and rare trips into town. Mark worked at adding a small room onto the back of the house. Nyla assumed Paul planned on using it for storage. Beatrice cooked. Randolph handled maintenance issues. Beatrice went from sneaking around with Mark to openly having sex with both him and Randolph. Though the three of them appeared to embrace this agreement, Nyla felt an undercurrent there. Like an imminent explosion awaited. Ava continued to entertain them every night with her music as well as her grandmother's job of being the group's seamstress.

The change between Ava and Paul came gradually—their stolen kisses turned to open affection; she sat where June usually sat at mealtime; and then Ava slept with Paul.

The first night it happened, Ava paused at Paul's door, looking over her shoulder and across the hall where Nyla lay on her top bunk. Her heart contracted in painful hope that Ava would change her mind and come back to the bunk room.

But she didn't. She stepped into Paul's room and closed the door.

Nyla watched that door for hours, but Ava never came back out.

The next night, Ava didn't look at Nyla as she went into Paul's room. Nyla gave it several minutes before climbing down from the top bunk. She tiptoed across the hall. She stared at their door. Whispering came through, followed by moans. Nyla moved closer, pressing her ear to the wood panels. She listened to their lovemaking.

The first few nights their noises didn't make her angry. It made her jealous. But then somehow it comforted her. She imagined being in that room with Ava instead of Paul. She imagined Ava wanted her in that room instead of Paul. She imagined Ava made those noises for her.

One night after listening, Nyla went back to her bunk. She stayed awake, staring at the peeling ceiling. Gradually, her eyes grew heavy. She slept.

The ladder up to her bunk creaked. A shift on Nyla's mattress woke her. Ava crawled in beside her. Nyla's heart stopped.

"Hi," Ava whispered.

"Hi back."

"Can I sleep here?" she quietly asked.

Nyla told herself to remain calm. "Of course."

Ava slid beneath the covers. She took Nyla's hand.

"Are you okay?" Nyla asked.

Ava nodded. "Why?"

"I don't know. Do you want to be there with Paul? He's not making you, is he?"

"It's good to share yourself. It's an unselfish act."

Nyla fell mute.

Ava pushed at the corners of Nyla's mouth with her index finger. "Smile."

Hesitantly, Nyla did.

Ava chuckled at the tentative compliance. She rested her forehead against Nyla's. They curled up facing each other. Nyla breathed in her scent—a mixture of their home-made soap, shampoo, and the wine from dinner.

"Did it hurt?" Nyla asked. "The first time?"

"Yes. But that's just my body adjusting and cleansing itself."

More of Paul's words.

"It got better the more we did it. Paul's been very gentle and patient. He knows how inexperienced I am." Ava shifted, kissing Nyla's forehead. "When are you?"

"When am I what?"

"Going to lose your virginity," she whispered.

"I...I don't know."

"Mark took an interest in you when you first arrived. Why don't you do it with him?"

Why did she have to "do it" with anybody?

"It's something to think about," Ava said.

"Did Paul tell you to say this to me?"

Ava didn't answer that question. "We all need a mate and to procreate. It's natural. I have Paul. Beatrice has

Randolph. Mark needs someone all his own. It's a suggestion."

*Suggestion.* Paul used that word with Nyla. He had a suggestion should she not begin contributing to the family. Was this Mark thing it? But she now contributed with the greenhouse. Not to mention all the time she cared for Karly. Did none of that matter?

Somehow, she didn't think it did.

Mating with Mark.

She wanted to throw up.

Nyla sat up. "I need to go to the bathroom."

Ava tugged her back down. She grinned, and suddenly Nyla didn't want to throw up anymore. She wanted to be there again, safe and warm, comforted by Ava's love.

Ava kissed her again, this time on the lips. Then she closed her eyes and snuggled in.

Nyla did not. She kept her eyes open, staring at Ava's face. She wanted to beg her to leave. To run far away and start a life of their own.

But she didn't because Ava would pick this place and Paul over Nyla. Until Ava picked Nyla first, she would do whatever was required of her.

Including the *suggestion.*

---

NYLA WOKE to find Paul standing in the doorway to the bunk room, staring hard at her and Ava sleeping on the top bunk.

Nyla's blood turned cold.

"Get down," he ordered. "Both of you."

Ava woke up then. So did Carrie, on the other side of the room, and Mark to the right.

Nyla's gut roiled. She pushed the covers back, not daring to look at Ava, and climbed down first with her friend behind. They stood beside each other, their heads down.

Paul stepped from the doorway, coming to stand in front of them. Even though he stood five-eight, he seemed to tower over them. He looked from Nyla to Ava, then back. "What were you two doing?"

"Just sleeping," Nyla quietly answered. She wanted to take Ava's hand. She wanted Ava to take hers. Whatever remarkable and good thing existed between last night was gone. They hadn't drifted back to reality on a slow wake, they'd been fired from a cannon to this spot in the bunk room where they stood barefoot on the hardwood floor.

"Whose idea was this?" Paul demanded.

"Mine," Ava murmured. Still, with her head bowed, she reached a tentative hand out but Paul refused the gesture.

"Nothing happened," Nyla whispered, humiliated that her father found them; mortified he reprimanded them; and embarrassed Carrie and Mark were in the room.

All for what, two friends sleeping together?

Yet, they were more than friends. *Paul* knew they were more than friends.

"Sarah's awake." Paul turned away. He strode from the bunk room, across the hall, and back into his room. Still, with her head down, Ava sheepishly followed.

Nyla watched Ava go to Sarah's crib and pick her up. Paul stepped up behind them. Ava turned. Paul stared silently into her eyes. Neither spoke. After a long moment, he put his forehead to hers and caressed his fingers down her cheek. Then he pressed a kiss to Sarah's head and walked from the room.

In the hallway he paused, looking into the bunk room at

Nyla. She waited for the same gentle acceptance that he showed Ava, but none came.

Instead, he took the stairs down.

The door opened. It closed.

A strange dread settled through Nyla. Though Paul didn't say it, repercussions were to come.

# ELEVEN

## LEAH

*Present Day*

IN THE EARLY MORNING HOURS, I finally manage to extract myself from her bed. Dazed, I walk across the hall back into the master suite. Walker sits in the corner chair, still dressed in his robe, a cup of coffee perched in his hand as he stares at the floor where he found Nyla.

He looks up at me.

"I'm sorry," I tell him again. "I've been in there on her bed staring at her for hours trying to wrap my brain around what happened."

"What did you come up with?"

"Nothing. My brain is frozen."

"Why did you stay in there?"

"She wouldn't let me go." I sit down on the edge of our bed. "She was uncharacteristically needy. I didn't know how to handle it."

He makes no response.

"I'm her mom," I say.

His jaw hardens. I note the frustration and anger in his expression. I go to him, kneeling on the floor next to his chair. Gently, I clasp his lower leg. "I'm as lost as you on this."

He studies my face for a long time. I wait patiently. I'm in a tough spot between an estranged daughter and a man I fiercely love. I don't want to lose either one.

Walker says, "I know you are her mother. You love her. You have longed for her. Now she's back with years unaccounted for. Her behavior is moody, erratic, and alarming. Based on what you told me, she was a challenging kid, but nothing like this."

"True."

"Leah, your daughter needs help. Something happened to her, and someone needs to figure out what it is. I don't know what Paul did to her, but she's broken."

# TWELVE
## NYLA

*Three Years Earlier*

NO REPERCUSSIONS CAME, not as Nyla expected. Paul did not physically or verbally chastise her beyond the original morning he found her and Ava in the same bed.

Ava, though, stopped talking to Nyla; stopped looking at Nyla; stopped everything involving Nyla. The rejection came worse than anything Paul did.

The bond Ava and Nyla shared didn't fade, it combusted. Nyla paid the price multiple times over with Ava's complete and utter avoidance of her. Unfortunately, it did nothing to deter Nyla's feelings. She loved Ava and felt convinced, with time, Ava would come back to her.

While she waited for that to happen, Nyla threw herself into gardening. She spent as many hours as possible in the greenhouse. It reminded her of the endless days and nights she stayed tucked away with Karly. Nyla felt invisible.

Summer rolled to winter. Nyla turned twenty.

Many things happened.

Randolph lost interest in Beatrice and focused all of his attention onto Carrie, now seventeen.

Beatrice and the child she had with Randolph moved into the bunk room.

Carrie and her child moved in with Randolph.

Paul began a new obsessive routine of washing Ava's long hair, combing it, smelling it, and wrapping it around his neck, his arms, and his head.

Paul also became fixated with their furniture. *Why do we need such frivolous things? We came here to get back to the basics. All we seem to do is accumulate more.*

What accumulation? They existed with the barest of necessities. Then one day Paul announced all of the pine furniture would be broken down and made into firewood. They kept mattresses, the picnic table to eat at, kitchenware, and cushions for the living room. That's it.

After that Paul became fanatical with privacy. *Privacy leads to secrets*, he said. *Secrets lead to deceit. Deceit breaks down trust. Trust is all a family truly needs.*

He asked Mark to remove all the doors in the house.

With all the rooms fully exposed, everything became open and free. At any given time, Nyla would see someone on the toilet, in the bathtub, in a room getting dressed, or... being intimate. She tried to ignore, to not see or hear or listen, but the absence of doors made it difficult.

She never once tried to ignore Paul and Ava's lovemaking, though. She looked forward to those nights and to listening to Ava's soft moans sifting across the hall.

Yes, no doors save for one. The room Mark built onto the back of the house contained a door, with a lock. Paul held the key to that lock. No one saw inside. Paul announced *It's there should we need it*. No one questioned him, out loud at least.

Though Nyla lost weight during the months of being on Paul's half rations, she hadn't—according to him—lost enough. So, half rations continued.

On one January morning, months after everything happened with Ava in the top bunk, Beatrice stepped into the greenhouse. Nyla acknowledged her entrance with a tiny smile. They had lived together for two full years and rarely held a conversation. All of their communication centered around passing *hellos* and *nice meal* and *do you have any dirty laundry?* Yet Nyla knew something so intimate as to what she sounded like while having sex with Mark.

"Hi," Beatrice greeted her. She wore her previously choppy red hair long, and like Nyla's hair, thin.

"Hi, back."

Beatrice walked over to the tomatoes, gently pressing them. Given everything that happened with Randolph moving onto Carrie, Beatrice acted so unbothered by the shift in dynamics. Like she took all new things in stride, including Randolph ditching her.

"How are things?" she asked.

"Okay, I guess."

"I was going to go with weird." She laughed.

Nyla laughed too. "Yeah. Weird."

"I mean, what's up with all the changes? Am I right?"

"There's been a lot. That's for sure."

They shared another smile.

Beyond the greenhouse, Randolph and Carrie strolled by with the kids trailing behind. Beatrice noted them before turning back to Nyla.

"Why do you stay?" Nyla asked. "Especially now that Randolph and Carrie are together."

"Well, it's certainly not because I'm madly in love with Mark." She pointed to a ripe tomato. "May I?"

"Sure."

Beatrice picked it, then took a bite. Nyla automatically looked for Paul. He didn't like it when they ate outside of meal time.

"Why do *you* stay here?" Beatrice asked. She narrowed her eyes. "And don't tell me it's because Paul is your father."

Nyla busied herself pruning a new growth she'd already pruned. She didn't want to answer that question.

"That's okay, forget I asked." Beatrice ate another bite of tomato. "Me? I'll stay until I feel it no longer makes sense. One can't argue with free room and board."

"That's right. I heard you used to live out of your car."

"I did, yes." Beatrice wandered around the greenhouse, stopping here and there to read labels, to touch, to smell. On a table sat the book June left titled *The Good and Bad Side of Herbs*. Idly, Beatrice flipped through it.

Her presence here felt both familiar and odd. Familiar like she knew her way around a little too well and odd like she wanted something, but Nyla didn't know what.

"What do you think of Paul?" Beatrice asked, not looking up from the book.

Again, Nyla glanced beyond the walls of the greenhouse, as if her father might hear.

She didn't know how to respond to that question. She opted for something neutral. "He's complicated, I guess. Aren't we all?"

"Complicated. Hm. Wouldn't you say 'sinister' better describes him?"

Sinister. Wow, what a creepy word. But something

ominous *had* been unlocked in Paul. Their family no longer contained a democracy. Paul ruled and no one appeared to mind.

Beatrice finished the last bite of the tomato. "Any idea what's in that room Mark built?"

"No. Why don't you ask Mark?"

"I did. He didn't reveal anything. I know it has working plumbing though."

"You mean like a bathroom?"

"I think so."

That didn't coincide with Nyla's previous thoughts it might be for storage.

"If you find out, let me know." Beatrice held up the book. "What's the 'bad?'"

It took Nyla a second to catch up with the change in topic. "There are a lot of plants and herbs considered poisonous."

"Like?"

"Well, sassafras causes hallucinations. Life root is connected to liver damage. Pennyroyal is linked to convulsions. Ephedra to high blood pressure. Calamus to an upset stomach. And many more."

Beatrice nodded beyond Nyla's shoulder to the back corner where June had sectioned off an area for her poison garden. Not too long ago, Nyla placed a stake in the dirt, painted with a black skull and crossbones.

According to June's journal, growing such rare plants challenged her. At first, Nyla considered trashing them but ended up adding to the garden items June already had but had never been able to grow.

The "bad."

"That's the infamous poison garden, isn't it?" Beatrice asked.

---

ONE WEEK LATER, Carrie died.

It happened in the early morning hours when the house slept. Randolph's scream woke the family.

Everyone hurried in to see him cradling Carrie, frantically scooping foam that gathered in her mouth. Someone turned on the overhead light. It illuminated the red rash covering Carrie's body and the dried blood stuck to her nose and ears.

On a small mattress in the corner, Little Carrie cried. Nyla hurried into the room and picked her up. She took her out into the hall where Beatrice hovered, silently looking in.

They made brief eye contact before Beatrice went into the room to Randolph. She knelt beside him, placing her hand on his back.

"She was pregnant," Randolph whispered, his voice full of tears.

*Pregnant?*

"Sh. Sh." Beatrice rubbed his back. "It's going to be okay."

Randolph turned away from Carrie and fell into Beatrice's arms.

Paul quietly moved into the room. He knelt beside Carrie and closed her eyes that were rimmed in red.

Ava shifted over next to Nyla. "Want me to take her?"

It was the first time Ava spoke directly to her since everything that happened. Nyla drank in her voice. "No, it's okay." She ran a hand down the child's back. Her crying lessened. "Did you know Carrie was pregnant?"

Shaking her head, Ava placed two hands over her stomach.

Softly, Nyla gasped. Her heart skipped a beat. "Wait a minute, are you...?"

Ava nodded. Tears filled her eyes as she looked back into the room at Carrie.

Mark knelt next to Paul. He studied Carrie's face. "What happened?"

"Looks like poisoning," Paul said.

Nyla's eyes snapped to Beatrice. Still holding a crying Randolph, she met her gaze across the room. Something knowing and dark passed across her face.

---

LIKE KARLY, they built a pyre and cremated Carrie on a freezing January day. Beatrice hovered around Randolph offering endless comfort.

Nyla wrestled with her knowledge and in the end, asked to speak privately with Paul.

They met in the greenhouse where Nyla showed him the area with skull and crossbones. "That's June's poison garden that I've been tending. Beatrice came in here a week or so ago asking me about it. I can't prove it, but I think she took clippings and killed Carrie."

Paul remained quiet as he moved to the rear of the greenhouse to study the poison garden. He didn't touch any of the plants, but he leaned down to read the labels.

"Also, she said some things that made me think she wasn't okay with Randolph choosing Carrie over her."

Still studying the plants, Paul asked, "Why did you keep this?"

"They're hard to grow. I like the challenge," she answered, not sure of the truth behind that statement. The moment she read the word "Bad" in the title of June's book, it sparked Nyla's curiosity.

Now she knew exactly what that word meant.

"Hard to grow and yet they thrive." Paul turned to look at her. "You've done a great job in here. I'm proud of you."

Nyla couldn't remember the last time Paul said something kind to her. "Thank you."

"You've also lost a lot of weight. You look much slimmer and healthy now."

She smiled. "Thank you, Paul." She glanced at the poison garden. "You don't want me to get rid of it then? I wasn't sure given what's happened."

"On the contrary. I like knowing something so deadly is steps away."

His comment unsettled Nyla.

"What else did Beatrice say?" Paul asked.

Nyla didn't know why she kept talking. Perhaps because this was the first real conversation she'd had with her father in forever. "She called you sinister."

"Did she now?" Paul gave her a closed-lip smile. He turned away, idly walking around the greenhouse. "I saw you holding Little Carrie. Are you feeling more comfortable with kids now?"

"I guess."

"I'd like you to become her mother now that her real one is gone."

Nyla did not like this request. "Okay, I can do that."

"Good. I'm not sure if you've heard but Ava is pregnant. Between that and Sarah, Ava has a lot on her plate. I need you to step up. You've thrived out here in this greenhouse but now I need more from you. Can you do that, Nyla?"

"Yes, of course. Whatever you need."

He finished walking around the greenhouse, coming to

stand in front of her. He placed a warm hand on her shoulder. "I knew I could count on you."

---

THAT NIGHT PAUL and Mark took Randolph outside to talk. When Randolph came back into the house, he went straight upstairs to pack his things.

Beatrice followed.

The next morning the two of them and their child were gone.

# THIRTEEN
## LEAH

*Present Day*

WALKER DEPARTED EARLY FOR WORK. Nyla avoided me the whole morning. I counted both things as a blessing. After last night's odd events, we all needed space.

I'm sitting on the couch in the living room, working on my laptop when Nyla walks in front of the windows, pushing a wheelbarrow full of gardening supplies she got from the shed in our side yard.

Curious, I go to the window to watch.

She's already sectioned off a portion of the backyard with string and wood stakes. She's dressed in a faded pair of denim overalls with a lightweight, long sleeve tee.

Kneeling, she begins digging up the ground, making a long and narrow row. She tucks peat moss down into the shallow dirt channel. Next, she takes tiny envelopes of seeds and studies them, deciding. She opens the one she wants and carefully places the seeds. She continues, doing another row and another. Five in all.

The whole time I stand here watching. She never expressed interest in gardening before. She's learned that from being with Paul.

She must feel my stare because she glances over her shoulder to the window where I stand. I give a little wave that she returns.

She seems content.

In the kitchen, I select a bottle of water from the refrigerator and walk it out to her. Though it's a chilly day, sweat glistens along her neck.

"Here, thought you might be thirsty." I hand her the water.

She takes the bottle. "I'm okay with tap. Bottled water is unnecessary."

"Just drink it, Nyla."

She does.

"What are you planting?" I ask.

"Lettuce, onions, potatoes, peas, and asparagus. They can stand the cooler temperatures of spring." She glances up as if just realizing something. "That's okay, isn't it? You don't mind I'm planting things?" She cringes. "I kind of dug up your yard, huh?"

I sit down on the grass. "It's okay. We have some lumber. We could frame it out into a bed."

She smiles. "Cool."

I love that she's doing this. It means she's staying. Or at least I hope it means that.

She puts the plastic bottle down and goes back to work. I note she's not wearing gloves. "You should put gloves on."

"No, thank you. I like feeling the earth."

Silently, I watch her. I always liked the idea of gardening, but every time I tried, it bored me. I'm a gardening shopper. I'll buy things, thinking I'll use them, and then they go into the shed. I'm glad Nyla's making use.

"Did Paul teach you how to do this?"

It's slight, but her relaxed shoulders stiffen. "No. I learned by reading and trying. Turned out I was pretty good at it."

"Makes me wish we would have been part of a community garden in Atlanta."

"I probably would've liked that."

From the potting soil bag, she scoops handfuls and gently layers them over the seeds.

"You look like you know what you're doing."

"With this, yes."

"With lots of things, I'm sure."

"One or two," she mumbles.

She continues working, moving on to sprinkling a light amount of herbal fertilizer. My gaze travels down her body. I think about seeing her naked body while she was skinny dipping and the wet marks in her bra... "Do you have a child?" I boldly ask.

She pauses in working. One dirty hand comes up, pressing into her breast. She stares at the garden. I've made her uncomfortable, but I need to know. "Do you?"

"Yes."

"How long ago?"

"Five months."

I suck in a breath. "Where is the baby now?"

Silence.

I don't regret asking. I can't keep walking on eggshells around her. I wait, staring at the side of her face. "You can talk to me. You ran from something to me. That means you trust me. Trust me now. Where have you been? What happened to you? Where is your baby?"

I expect her to stand, fire off some comment, then stomp away.

Instead, she looks at me with a gaze full of so much warning it comes across as threatening. Her voice is measured when she says, "I'm out here gardening, actually relaxing, and then you had to come out and ruin it. I have nothing to say to you about anything. I didn't come here because I trust you or ran to you. I didn't even realize you'd be here. But you are. You can either accept that I'm back or you can keep prying. Keep prying though, and I'll leave again. This time for good. Now, *Leah*, leave me the fuck alone so I can get back to relaxing."

# FOURTEEN
## NYLA

*Three Years Earlier*

IF THERE'S one thing Nyla admitted about her mother, she put on a fabulous Christmas. From a fresh tree to home-made goodies, to vibrantly wrapped gifts, to stockings and music and warm cider, Nyla did miss her mother's elaborate holiday.

The season had passed already but Nyla didn't see any reason why they couldn't celebrate it anyway and have Christmas in January.

She surveyed the common room with its cushions for furniture and pine burning in the fireplace. She wanted to do something, anything to recognize the belated day.

It didn't have to be big. Just something.

Plus, Paul did say he wanted her to do more.

He and Mark would be back in a few hours from walking the property.

Nyla found Ava outside playing with the children.

"What do you say we surprise the men and decorate for a belated Christmas?"

Ava brightened.

Inside they came up with a game plan for themed crafts, baked goods, and warm wine. They worked fast to ready the place. When two hours later heavy footsteps tread the porch, Nyla, Ava, and the children hurried to gather. They vibrated with excitement.

The front door opened. Paul stepped in first. He paused when he noticed the paper snowflake decorations taped along the walls. He looked at the plate of ginger cookies sitting center on the picnic table. In the corner, a radio played cheery music.

Mark came in behind Paul. Mark noticed the fireplace where the girls hung socks stitched with each person's name. "Not bad," Mark told them, smiling.

Nyla held her breath, waiting for Paul's reaction, but none came.

"Merry January Christmas!" Little Carrie chirped.

Two-year-old Sarah ran over and handed Paul a drawing of Santa. Paul took the drawing, but he didn't look at it.

Instead, he looked at Nyla. "I thought you knew that I don't believe in holidays."

Nyla's smile fell away.

So did Ava's.

"Take all of this down. Now." Paul walked back outside.

Mark gave both of them a commiserating look before following Paul.

The door closed. Ava shrunk in on herself. Nyla didn't know what to say. Ava didn't either. Instead, she moved quickly, yanking down all the decorations and throwing them into the fire. Sarah started crying. So did Little Carrie. Nyla felt like crying along with the girls.

When Ava finished, she charged upstairs leaving Nyla alone to tend to both crying kids.

---

LATE THAT NIGHT after the children slept and the men dozed off, Ava tiptoed from the master bedroom. Quietly, she took the stairs down, and even more quietly she opened the front door.

Nyla didn't waste a second following.

On the porch she found Ava sitting with her knees drawn up and a blanket wrapped around her.

"May I?" Nyla whispered, nodding to the spot beside her.

"Sure." She opened the blanket. Nyla eagerly sat down.

They didn't speak. They simply took in the dark, frigid night with the winter sky clear and full of bright stars. The smell of their fire from earlier lingered in the air. Ava seemed pensive.

But the next few minutes unfolded like a dream. Ava placed her head on Nyla's shoulder. "If you could live anywhere, where would you go?"

"That's easy. My grandmother's log cabin in Georgia. It's in the mountains and overlooks a river. There's even a rowboat."

"That sounds ideal."

"Maybe one day we'll go."

"I'd like that." Ava breathed deeply. "Do you remember when we got in trouble for being in your bed?"

Nyla nodded. Of course, she remembered.

"I'm sorry that all happened," Ava said.

"Me too. And I'm sorry about earlier. I didn't know Paul doesn't celebrate holidays."

"That's okay." Ava shifted, moving closer. Nyla opened her arm. Ava snuggled in. She asked, "Do you ever think about leaving?"

Nyla stilled. "I did a few times, but I haven't thought of it lately."

"Why?"

"I wouldn't leave without you." Nyla shifted, looking at Ava's face. "Do you want to leave?"

Sadly, her friend smiled. "I can't, especially now that I'm pregnant. Where would I go? I have no one. I'd be homeless."

"You'd have me."

"It's not so bad here, I guess. I liked it a lot more when the house was full."

Nyla liked it a lot more without so many people. She liked the intimacy of just her and Ava. "I liked it a lot more with furniture."

Ava chuckled. "I think it would be amazing if you got pregnant too. Then we can go through it together."

Nyla grew quiet.

"I mean, it's just a suggestion."

*Suggestion.* There it was again.

Ava straightened up. She turned to Nyla. "What do you think?"

One tiny inch separated their faces. A small shift forward and they would be kissing.

Ava grabbed Nyla's cheeks. "Get pregnant. Have sex with Mark." Her grip on Nyla's face tightened. "Please, Nyla. *Please.* I can't do this by myself."

Nyla stared hard into Ava's eyes. She would do anything her friend wanted, even if Paul planted this suggestion.

So, that night she lost her virginity on a mattress to a man old enough to be her father in a room with no door.

# FIFTEEN
## LEAH

*Present Day*

THERE IS no way I'm telling Walker about my encounter with my daughter. It'll just add fuel to the already fragile situation.

It worries me how many things I'm not telling him.

I spend the rest of the day trying to finish my work. To say I'm distracted puts it lightly. I parented Nyla with a firm hand. Maybe too firm. I also spoiled her. She had so much while growing up, more than needed. I made mistakes. I know this. I was trying to make up for being a single parent.

I was trying to make up for the fact I asked Paul, her favorite person in the world, to leave.

Paul had this charisma that drew people in. It drew me, in the beginning. It took years to realize he used that mesmerizing charm to control. He played mind games. He talked big. He loved being loved. He knew how to make people feel that love also, and acceptance. He had the uncanny ability to get what he wanted, always. He could convince people of pretty much anything.

He was also always "finding himself" which meant he lived off of me.

At first that didn't bother me. His dreaming inspired me. Then it annoyed me. But what troubled me was how he talked about other people. It was always in this dark enthralling voice.

*Did you see the way he responded to my words?*

*I had her eating out of my hand.*

*I could've asked that old man to sign over his bank account and he would have.*

It made me wonder what he had talked me into over the years. He left much quieter and quicker than I imagined. Then again, I did give him half of my retirement and bought him out of his half of our Atlanta condo. My mother told me I was a fool to give him so much of my money, especially after he had lived off of me for a decade.

I didn't care. I wanted him out of my life, even though he'd always be in it because of our daughter.

"I'm sorry."

I'm sitting in the corner chair of the master suite when I hear Nyla's soft voice. She stands hesitantly in the doorway still dressed in her denim overalls.

In the past, those two words—so rarely said by her—used to instantly soften me. Now, they work in the opposite. She can't just treat me like crap and then expect it to all go away.

Not anymore.

"You hurt me," I tell her. "I know I was prying, but it's only because you're so locked up. I only want to know you're okay. You can't say things like that to me. It's disrespectful and harmful."

"I know."

For several long seconds, I study her while she does everything *but* look at me. She looks at the bed, the dressers, the door to the bathroom, the closet...

When she finally does redirect her gaze to me, I say, "I like that you're making a garden." It's not the same as "apology accepted" but it'll do.

She smiles a little. "Thanks."

"Will you at least tell me if the baby is safe?"

A beat goes by. "Yes, the baby is safe."

I don't like that she hesitated. "Because if the baby isn't, I can help."

"Evie's fine, okay?"

*Evie.* I have a granddaughter. "Okay."

Again, she looks all around the room. I get the distinct feeling she wants to ask me something, but she's not sure how. "What is it?"

"I thought I saw an old blue truck drive by just now. Do any of your neighbors have one?"

"I don't know. Why?"

"Just curious." She slides her hands into the pockets of her overalls. She looks down at the floor. "Does, um, Paul know where this place is?"

"He came here once with me to visit my mother. It was way back before you were born. That's it. He doesn't know the address. He probably doesn't even remember where it is. It's hard to find. All of the houses up and down this mountain are. They're tucked in and hidden away."

I close the lid on my laptop. She keeps standing in the doorway, now fidgeting with her thumbnail. I study her. Something is troubling her and it has nothing to do with what happened between the two of us outside in the garden.

"Nyla, are you worried Paul will come here?"

Her chest rises in a deep breath. She nibbles the inside of her cheek. She does another one of those visual journeys around the room.

"Nyla?"

Her eyes come back to meet mine. "Everything's fine. Forget I asked." She turns away. "I'm going to take a shower."

---

WALKER GETS HOME LATE, well after Nyla and I ate and she went to bed. He rarely, if ever, gets home late.

I'm sitting at the kitchen table, sipping a glass of merlot, and looking out the bank of windows that overlook the backyard and the river beyond, both glowing faintly in the moon. My brain spins.

*What exactly is Nyla afraid Paul will do?*

*Who is the father of her baby?*

*Where is the baby?*

*She came here because she thought the house would be empty. Why does she need an empty house?*

Walker disengages the alarm code, comes in through the garage door, then re-engages. I listen to his feet shuffle down the hallway.

"Hi." He steps into the kitchen. "You didn't have to wait up."

Yes, I did. He's crazy if he thinks we're not going to talk.

He puts an envelope on the table. "Found this taped to our front door. It's from that elderly couple that lives directly across from us."

"Bill and Edna."

"Yeah. They've invited us to a cookout tomorrow night."

Idly, I look at the invitation. "That's nice."

Walker sits down across from me. "I'm going to Atlanta on business."

"Oh. When?"

"Tomorrow."

It's not unusual for him to go to Atlanta on business. In truth, it's welcome news. But, "Tomorrow is Saturday."

He takes my hand. "I know. I'm going to meet up with a couple of friends too. I'll be gone a week, then I'll be back."

"Do you want to talk about what happened?"

"I said what I wanted to say. She needs help."

"I know that."

"Me being away will be good. You two need mother-daughter time."

I finish off my wine, stand, and take the glass to the sink. I wash it a little too forcefully and place it in the drainer to dry.

I don't know why I'm suddenly irritated with him. Maybe because I'd love some advice. Something other than "she needs help."

# SIXTEEN
# NYLA

*Three Years Earlier*

NYLA HATED how Mark spooned her every night. She liked her space. She also instantly became pregnant.

*Look at that*, Paul said when he found out. *I didn't even have to make the suggestion.*

Whatever.

Now, with both young women pregnant, the rules quickly came:

- No leaving the property
- No eating outside of the prescribed meal plan
- No celebrating holidays, including birthdays
- Anyone pregnant must exercise once per day
- Anyone pregnant must not gain more than twenty-five pounds
- No postpartum depression is allowed
- Babies must be breastfed for six months

- All children will be moved into the spare bedroom at the age of one
- No sex after birth until six weeks has transpired
- All births will be managed at home in the tub

*This is for your good as well as your baby's* Paul and Mark told them as they presented the rules written on the chalkboard where the chores used to be listed.

That chore list plagued Nyla when she first arrived. It slowly dwindled as people either left or died. Now the chores came implied:

Women—cooking, cleaning, laundry, childcare, sewing.

Men—yard work, maintenance, errands.

Back to the rules, Nyla studied the bulleted list. For the most part, they already did several of the items. She knew next to nothing about pregnancy, but the other rules sounded plausible. She wanted a healthy body and baby.

She zeroed in on the words "babies" and "children."

Her body chilled.

She and Ava would be expected to have more.

---

ON A SPRING DAY during Nyla's first trimester and Ava's second, they slipped into lightweight sweaters and went for their daily prescribed walk. The children—Sarah, now nearly two and a half, and Little Carrie, four and a half —skipped along in front of them.

A frigid winter gave way to an instantly thawed spring. The sun glared brightly, filling the air with the promise of warm weather to come.

The sound of a rifle popped through the woods. The men left an hour ago to practice shooting.

The women followed the noise. As they grew closer, they each grabbed the hand of a child. Up ahead through the woods, the men stood side by side with their backs to the women, aiming at bottles they'd set up.

Paul fired. Glass spewed in all directions. He and Mark shared a triumphant look.

"Hello," Ava called out, sweetly.

Paul and Mark turned. They both smiled. Paul beckoned them. "Want to try?"

Ava shot Nyla a surprised look.

"Sure." An unexpected spurt of excitement danced through Nyla.

"It's okay for the baby?" Ava hesitantly asked.

The men laughed. "Of course." They waved the women over.

"It's good to learn how to defend yourself." Paul pointed for the two little girls to sit behind them on a downed tree. "You press your hands to your ears when we start firing, okay?"

The girls nodded.

Paul gave Ava his rifle and Mark gave Nyla his.

The men hovered behind the women, demonstrating what Paul called the "Hasty Sling" method. "Using your rifle sling to create tension between your arm and the rifle allows you to steady your aim," Paul instructed. "Hold the rifle out with your right hand and let the sling hang down. Place your left arm through the opening, above the sling, and below the rifle. Raise that arm up and behind the sling. Now slip your hand back over, grasp the forestock of the rifle, then shoulder it. Do you feel how the tension steadies your hold?"

Ava and Nyla nodded.

"See how it crosses your chest here?" Mark added,

trailing his finger along the sling. "See how it wraps around the outside of your arm?"

"Yes," Nyla said.

"Now, align your sight with the target," Paul continued. "Keep both eyes open and make the aiming time brief. Control your breathing. When you're ready, draw a deep breath and exhale halfway. You'll hold the rest of your breath as you squeeze the trigger. Don't jerk it, simply apply slow and steady pressure. After the bullet fires, continue to squeeze to avoid jolting the gun."

"Ready?" Mark asked.

Nyla's heart raced. Eagerly, she nodded. Mark stepped back, as did Paul. Nyla fired at a green bottle some ten yards away. It shattered upon impact. She gasped with delight.

Ava didn't fire.

Mark pointed at a red can fifteen yards away. Nyla pulled the trigger. It flew into the air.

Ava still didn't fire.

Mark pointed to a yellow cardboard box twenty yards away. Nyla sighted it. The bullet whizzed out. The box caught air.

Ava still didn't fire.

Mark pointed to a clear glass mason jar twenty-five yards away. Nyla aimed. Glass spewed through the air.

Ava still didn't fire.

Exhilarated, Nyla lowered the rifle. She looked over at Ava, frozen in place, trembling, still holding the weapon up.

Nyla looked at Paul who nodded approvingly. She beamed under his favorable gaze. She opened her mouth, about to tell Ava it was okay, when he said, "Shoot the gun, Ava. Now."

Her trembling body shook. Her breath stuttered. She

fired the gun. It jerked hard in her arms. She stumbled back. The bullet disappeared into the trees.

Paul grasped her shoulders. He resituated the rifle in her arms. "Focus. Deep breath. Think about someone who has made you angry. Feel that anger in your stomach. Allow that anger to travel to your hands. Welcome it building inside of you. Transfer that anger to the gun."

Ava's shaking body quivered. She cried. "Please don't make me. Please."

"It's okay," Nyla told her, looking at her father. "Right, Paul? She doesn't want to."

With a deep sigh, Paul took the gun from Ava. She collapsed in his arms. Reluctantly, he held her.

Mark stepped up behind Nyla. He wrapped his arms around her, kissing her neck and groping her swollen breasts. "You firing that gun was hot," he whispered.

Embarrassed, Nyla moved his hands away.

"Shall we try thirty yards?" Mark asked.

Nyla looked at Paul, still holding a crying Ava. Paul nodded.

Mark showed her how to reload the rifle. Then he jogged into the trees to set up a target at thirty yards.

"Shoot at him," Paul said.

"*What?*" Nyla gasped.

Paul moved Ava away. He nodded to Mark way in the woods. "Shoot at him."

"I'm not going to shoot at Mark."

"Why not? I didn't say hit him. I said to shoot *at* him."

Confused, Nyla looked at Ava.

"Don't look at her." Paul stepped into Nyla's face. "Look at me. Sure, Mark's the father of your baby, but you don't love him. Right?"

Nyla gave a jerky nod.

"You only got pregnant because Ava asked. Right?"

Nyla swallowed.

"You hold no affection for Mark. Just a minute ago he boldly felt you up. You didn't want that, did you?"

"No."

Paul stepped to the side. "Shoot at him. Let him know you're the boss."

Another swallow. Nyla looked through the woods at Mark. "No." She took the rifle off. "I'm not shooting at Mark."

Paul jerked the gun from her hands. He lifted it, sighted it, and shot. Wood splintered only a yard or so from Mark. He yelled. Paul shoved the gun back into Nyla's hands. "You told me you trusted me."

"I do."

"Then why are you still questioning me? If I tell you to do something, then do it. I thought you were stronger than this." Paul turned away.

Stunned, she watched him walk past the little girls, taking the path back to the house. Something built inside of her. It gathered in her core, fisting, twisting, transforming into ugliness. Just a minute ago she'd been beaming under his favorable gaze. Not now. Now she was mad.

*Think about someone who has made you angry.*

She lifted the gun.

*Feel that anger in your stomach.*

She waited until Paul reached twenty yards away.

*Allow that anger to travel to your hands.*

Beside her, Ava softly pleaded.

*Welcome it building inside of you.*

Mark ran toward her.

*Transfer that anger to the gun.*

Nyla took a breath. She fired.

ALMOST A YEAR HAD GONE by since Mark built the room onto the back of the house with the only door, yes, but also with a lock.

*It's there if we need it,* Paul had said.

Even though it had plumbing, Nyla kept assuming it would be for storage. Or a guest should one arrive. Now, she knew differently.

The room was there to punish.

# SEVENTEEN

## LEAH

*Present Day*

WALKER IS UP and gone before Nyla awakes.

I linger in bed, dozing here and there.

The smell of breakfast brings me out of my room. I find my daughter downstairs in the kitchen, dressed in a robe, the radio on to a classic rock station as she makes pancakes.

When she looks up and sees me, the tiniest of smiles creases her face. "Good morning."

"Good morning."

"Pecan pancakes sound good?"

"Yes."

She nods to the coffee pot. "All ready when you are."

I pour a cup. "Walker's gone to Atlanta on business. He'll be back in a week or so."

"Okay."

With my mug, I sit down at the kitchen island and watch her cook. "We've been invited to a cookout tonight. You interested?"

"Where?"

"Straight across the river at Bill and Edna's place."

"Is that the old couple I shocked with my skinny dipping?"

"Yes."

She glances out the window toward their property. "How long would we be gone?"

"As long as we want, I guess."

She flips a pancake.

"I'd like to go and bring my daughter . . . even if you didn't come here for me." I speak the last part in a teasing tone.

She cuts me an amused look that I'm happy to see. "Okay, I guess."

"Thanks."

We eat breakfast. We chat. We busy ourselves for the day. I work some, even though its Saturday. She stays outside, spending some time walking up and down the driveway. At one point she sits on the front porch steps and just stares at the mountain road on the other side of the trees like she's waiting for someone.

Or looking for someone.

It's the second time I've seen her do that.

Eventually, she moves to the back yard where she fiddles with her garden.

When I ask her to help me dust and vacuum the house, she doesn't hesitate to do as I ask. She even makes a bean salad for the cookout. It's a fairly normal afternoon.

Until I decide to do laundry.

I grab her hamper from the bathroom. Downstairs in the laundry room, I sort clothes. At the bottom of her pile, I find the sheets I put on her bed the first day she arrived. They smell of urine.

My first inclination is to ask her about it. My second is to wash the sheets and pretend I didn't see anything. My third thought is to put it all back where I found it.

I go with the last. I don't want to embarrass her.

But as I walk the hamper back upstairs, it doesn't escape me that my twenty-three-year-old daughter wet her bed.

Just like she used to do as a child when she was terrified something would happen.

# EIGHTEEN
## NYLA

*Three Years Earlier*

FOR ONE WHOLE WEEK, Nyla stayed locked away in a windowless room with a single mattress, a toilet, and a sink. One bare bulb provided the only light. Without access to the sun, Nyla couldn't judge time passing. The days came in a mindless blur of endless captivity.

Ava brought meals. She refused to make eye contact with Nyla. Refused to speak to her. Refused to acknowledge she existed.

Paul drove those actions. Still, it stung.

Nyla waited for Ava to whisper a word. She waited for Ava to sneak a visit outside of the approved times. She waited for a tender touch. She waited on Ava to do anything that would break Paul's rules, but she didn't.

Nyla waited on Mark to challenge Paul. But Mark never showed. He was fine with the mother of his child being locked away, isolated, and punished.

Paul held ultimate control over everyone and everything.

She fought against the pull of the room as it dragged her into an emotional darkness. She tried willing anger and rebellion instead. Unfortunately, it did not work.

On the seventh day, the door opened. With his feet braced wide, Paul folded his arms. He radiated dark energy. Nyla cried. She'd been sufficiently beaten down. She wanted out of this room.

"You could've killed me," he spoke.

"I know. I'm sorry."

"I'm not sure you've learned your lesson."

Her heart paused. "I have. I promise I have."

"I don't get that. Your demeanor says otherwise." He looked around the small area. He sniffed. "Did you piss the mattress?"

"Yes." Nyla flushed. It happened to her a few times over the years—as a kid and even as a teenager—from stress, fear, and nerves. "I'll clean it. I promise."

"Fear is a powerful human emotion. It creates awareness. When you're scared, it forces you into your current moment. It makes you truly present. That's what you're feeling now—fear. Allow it in. Accept it. Feel it."

Nyla swallowed. She prayed he didn't close that door. She couldn't do another minute in there.

"Maybe I ask too much of you. You showed such potential in living this life. You pleased me but your latest actions greatly disappoint me."

Desperate, she crawled across the room and knelt at his feet. "Please forgive me."

For a long moment, he studied her. She held very still, looking up into his face. She needed him to be happy with her again.

He sighed. "Fine. You are forgiven. You may leave the room."

"Thank you." Tentatively, she touched his lower leg. "Thank you."

"You've developed a particular skill set with the greenhouse. I want you to focus on that. Grow new things. Experiment. Surprise me with something that proves your worth."

Nyla nodded.

Over the next several weeks, she worked hard at blending back in. She tended her plants. She did her chores. She focused on growing a healthy baby. She followed every rule without incident.

Mark feigned ignorance at what happened. Not once did he mention the locked room. Not once did he thank her for not shooting at him. No, he stayed connected to Paul's side. The two of them did everything together.

Ava barely spoke. Nyla's punishment demonstrated Paul's position and power. Even Sarah and Little Carrie remained quieter than usual.

―――――

DURING NYLA'S second trimester and Ava's third, they stood side by side in the kitchen preparing the evening meal. After Nyla's time in isolation, she thought things would go back to normal between her and Ava. But nothing had. They barely spoke.

As Nyla peeled potatoes, and Ava snapped beans, Little Carrie stood on a wood platform, washing apricots. Sarah sat on the kitchen floor playing with the wooden blocks that Mark made her. Outside the kitchen window, Paul pushed a manual mower while Mark raked the loose grass. Both men glistened in the late afternoon summer sun.

Nyla studied Mark with an unbiased eye. At over six feet he looked strong with muscles that pressed against his gray T-shirt. He still shaved his head every morning and his beard grew a bit grayer. She wouldn't describe him as handsome, but she still thought he had a kind face.

In contrast, Paul's lean body appeared almost bony. He wore his long black hair in a braid with a red bandana tied around his head. Paul did not have a kind face. He did however have a commanding one that matched the way he carried himself.

Once upon a time, Nyla admired her father. She wanted to be like him. She would have moved mountains to follow him.

Now though she simply thought of him as Paul: a man not to be messed with.

Finished with the potatoes, Nyla placed them in a bowl and turned toward the sink right as Ava smacked Little Carrie on the back of the head.

"No." Ava pointed her finger. "Bad girl." She snatched the apricots from the little girl. "Spit it out. Now."

Little Carrie's face blazed red. She spat an apricot into the sink. "I'm sorry," she muttered. "I'm so hungry."

Ava yanked her down off the stool.

Nyla stepped forward. "Ava..."

Her friend ignored her. Ava leaned down in Little Carrie's face. "You know the rules. No eating between meals. Do you want to go to the isolation room?"

Tears filled Little Carrie's eyes. "No."

"Then you better never do that again. If I see you sneaking food, I will tell Paul. Do you hear me?"

Little Carrie's bottom lip wobbled. "Yes, I hear you."

Ava pointed. "Now take Sarah and go outside and get the laundry off the line."

The little girl grabbed Sarah and hurried from the house.

Nyla stayed rooted to her spot, dumbfounded. She'd never seen Ava act like that.

Her friend went back to prepping the beans. Nyla kept staring at the side of her face. Tense seconds ticked by. Nyla wanted to say something, but nothing came.

Ava threw the beans down. She turned on Nyla. "What?" she snapped.

Nyla's mouth opened. It closed.

"This is all your fault," Ava said. "If you wouldn't have acted out, we wouldn't be under such strict rules."

The rules existed way before she "acted out." She was about to say as much when Ava's water broke.

# NINETEEN

## LEAH

*Present Day*

COME LATE AFTERNOON, Nyla strolls into the kitchen wearing the green dress I bought her. She's put on mascara and lip gloss from my vanity, loosely wrapped a long white scarf around her neck, and chose tiny gold hoop earrings. Her buzzed hair only serves to accentuate her features, almost giving her an exotic look.

"You look very pretty," I tell her.

"Thank you."

With the bean salad, we walk down to the river. Our rowboat floats in its usual spot, tied to the small dock.

When we used to come here to visit my mother, we took this boat out all the time. It holds nothing but good memories. We never argued during those adventures. We simply enjoyed it. One time I jokingly told my mother the boat was Switzerland—a nice neutral place.

She'd said, *then you two need to do more rowing.*

Together we board the boat and row the short distance

across the calm water to the other side. After tying off at Bill and Edna's dock, we take the backyard up to their home. As we do the sound of laughter and chatter fills the air. We come through a gap in the trees to see their back deck filled with people.

Beside me, Nyla stops walking.

I do as well. "What's wrong?"

"I thought it was just going to be us."

"Yeah, me too."

"Who are all these people?"

"Neighbors, I guess."

"You don't know?"

"Not really. Some of them look familiar." I start walking again. "Come on. It'll be okay."

Nyla moves close to me. We approach the deck and take the steps up. Edna's at the top, grinning. "Hi Leah, welcome!"

"Thanks for the invite." I inhale. "Whatever's on the grill smells great."

"Ribs and chicken."

I nod to Nyla who grips the salad like it's a security blanket. "We brought salad. This is Nyla, by the way. My daughter."

"Hi, Nyla. I do believe we informally met already." Edna winks as she reaches for the bowl. Nyla reluctantly hands it over before moving even closer to me. "Walker coming?"

"He's in Atlanta on business."

"Well, you tell him I say hi. Now, can I get you a beverage?" Edna asks. "We have everything from lemonade to iced tea to soda to beer to wine to the hard stuff."

I look at Nyla. But she doesn't return my look. She's

frozen in place, her eyes studying every single person crammed onto the deck.

"Lemonade for both of us. Thank you." While Edna walks off, I look back at my daughter.

"I want to go home," she says.

"But we just got here."

"I don't care. I want to go home."

"Nyla—"

"I WANT TO GO HOME!"

The deck quiets. Everyone turns to look. My face flushes with embarrassment. I grab her hand and yank her down the steps like she's a kid throwing a temper tantrum and not a grown woman. At the bottom stair, I let go and keep walking. Behind me, people gradually begin talking again. I don't look back, but I know she's hurrying to keep up.

At the boat, I climb in. She does as well. I untie and row us fast and hard over to our dock. I re-tie and get out. I wait until I'm back in my home until I whirl on her. "What the hell is wrong with you?"

I expect her to yell back. Instead, she races upstairs and slams her door.

*Oh hell no...* I charge after her. Anger boils inside of me. There is so much that wants to fly off of my tongue— nothing good and all most definitely damaging. I take a breath. I tell myself to calm down, but it doesn't work.

When I reach her room, I'm ready to barge in but the sound of her quiet sobbing stops me.

Never, not even as a little girl, did my daughter cry. There was anger, sure. Drama, yes. Yelling, all the time, but never tears. And definitely not sobbing.

My God, I don't know what to do.

I don't know how to help my daughter.

# TWENTY

# NYLA

*Two Years Earlier*

AVA GAVE birth to a stillborn baby boy.

Paul wrapped the baby in a white cloth. As with Karly and Carrie, they built a pyre.

Ava sobbed while Nyla held her.

*I knew something was wrong,* she wailed. *I didn't feel the baby move for weeks.*

Paul lost it. *That's not something you keep to yourself!* he screamed. It was the first—and only time—he raised his voice.

Paul blamed Nyla. He blamed Mark. He blamed Little Carrie and Sarah. He blamed Ava. He never once blamed himself.

Nyla didn't know where the fault landed. Sometimes these things happened. But if responsibility should be placed, she one hundred percent blamed him.

Over the next several weeks, the home curdled into

something monstrous. Paul supervised every word, every action, every look, everything.

A new rule appeared on the board.

- If a baby is born dead, the mother must get pregnant as soon as possible

A calendar went up with the date marked when Ava would be able to try again for another baby.

Nobody was allowed to go beyond the yard. No more walks in the woods occurred. Certainly, no trips to the creek happened. Not even Paul went into town for the usual run of supplies. Which meant the grain and bean stock dwindled. Meals consisted of fruit and vegetables only. Everyone lost weight. Nyla worried about her baby.

The calendar ticked down. At week six, Ava's cries filled the house as Paul forced her to make another baby. Nyla wanted to run across the hall and throw Paul off of her, but Mark held Nyla in place.

Ten days later, Paul proudly announced Ava's second pregnancy.

One day after that on a pretty fall afternoon, Nyla gave birth to a small, healthy baby girl. Paul allowed Nyla to name her. She picked Danae, after her own middle name.

Paul marked the calendar when Nyla would be expected to begin making a second baby.

---

FROM STRESS or lack of nutrition or both, Ava lost her hair. It came out in long blond clumps. With that came another rule:

- All female heads are to be shaved once per
  month

If Ava couldn't keep hair, none of them should have it, including the children.

Another rule:

- If we can't produce it, we don't need it

Translation: if Nyla couldn't grow it, they wouldn't eat.

---

FALL MOVED INTO WINTER. Nyla turned twenty-one.

Ava did not recover from her first baby's death. She withdrew from everyone. She barely ate. She lost weight.

Nyla needed to do something. She pled with Mark. "Please talk to Paul. Ava is not doing well."

"Ava is healing," Mark replied. "She's following her own path. Just be grateful you're not having the same problems."

Nyla stared in stupefaction. "Healing? She's not healing. She's lost her hair. She's too skinny. Have you seen her skin? It's gray. You call that 'healing'?" Nyla shouted. She broke so many rules right now, but she didn't care. "Paul forced himself on her and you did nothing. You held me down so I couldn't help. She's pregnant again because of him and he doesn't even care. Why get her pregnant then? If he cared, he'd go into town and get us some protein and grains. Hell, if he cared he'd have a kind word or look for her. He acts like she's no longer here!"

Paul's footsteps moved up the stairs. He entered their room. His hand latched onto her arm in a vice grip. He wrenched Nyla around. A cold hard slap landed across her face.

"You know nothing about anything," he spat.

The slap failed to control her. Instead, it ratcheted up her ire. "You think you're so powerful and in control? You are nothing. Ava lost her baby and you don't even care. All you care about is your stupid rules."

His hand came back, this time across the other side of Nyla's face.

"I'm leaving!" she screamed. "I'm taking Ava and the children. I am leaving, and you cannot stop me." Nyla shoved past him.

Paul grabbed her. She kicked and screamed and punched. "Let me go!" she yelled.

At the top of the stairs, he swung her forward. She stumbled down, catching herself. He grabbed her again and dragged her through the house past Ava and the children.

He unlocked the isolation room, flung her inside, and slammed the door. Nyla pounded the door. "Let me out!"

Paul's voice came quiet, menacing. "You want to leave? Go. But you are not taking anyone with you. Not even your baby. If you try, I will find you. I promise."

# TWENTY-ONE
## LEAH

*Present Day*

IN THE MORNING I'm sitting at the kitchen table, having coffee and staring out the bank of windows to the garden Nyla put in. Beyond that, the river twinkles as the sun makes its first appearance of the day. My mind drifts back to last night. I stood outside of Nyla's room, quietly listening to her cry. I tried her doorknob, finding it locked. Eventually, she grew quiet. I hoped she fell asleep.

Behind me, soft footsteps shuffle in.

Nyla goes to the coffee pot.

Without looking at her, I ask, "Do you blame me?"

"For what?"

"For anything, for everything."

"I don't know," she mumbles. "Maybe."

I turn in my chair to look at her. With swollen eyes and a splotchy face, she does not look like she slept. "I'm just trying to figure out why you ran away all those years ago.

Was it really that bad with me that you couldn't even leave a proper note or call to tell me that you were okay?"

"It doesn't matter. It's all in the past." With her mug, she starts to walk from the kitchen. But I'm not having that. We need to talk.

"No, it's *not* in the past. It's here in front of us, Nyla. I know that I was never the mom you wanted, but I did my best."

"I know you did."

"Do you? Because it sure doesn't feel that way."

"How does it feel?"

"Like you're angry."

"I'm not angry. But I understand you're questioning if there was more you could have done. I think maybe we're too similar. Don't they say that you fight with the child most like you?"

Sadly, I smile. "Yes, they do they say that."

We're both quiet for a moment. She opts not to leave the kitchen and instead slides up onto an island stool. It encourages me to continue. I get up from the table and choose a stool at the opposite end of the island, giving her space to leave if she wants.

"I've thought a lot about you over the years," I say, "analyzing your childhood and what I could or should have done differently. Bottom line, I think I was caught up in this image of what a mother and daughter should be. Yet, that was never us, and I never fully understood that." I chuckle a little. "You came out of my womb in no need of me."

She frowns. "That's not true."

"You and I both know it is," I tease.

We share a smile that gradually fades.

She sips her coffee. "I'm sorry I embarrassed you in

front of your friends. The crowd overwhelmed me. I freaked out."

"I get that. But all you need to do is communicate with me."

"I thought I did."

"Screaming isn't communicating."

She winces. "Yeah, that was a little over the top."

She seems approachable. It gives me the confidence to admit, "I want to know what the past five years of your life have been like, but I don't want to press my luck. I never know when you'll clam up on me, or get angry, or cry..." I leave that last word dangling out there. I want her to know that I heard her.

Nyla takes a sip of her coffee. "I'm not ready to tell you everything, but I can tell you some."

# TWENTY-TWO

## NYLA

*Two Years Earlier*

UNLIKE THE LAST time that Paul put Nyla in the isolation room, this time it did not quell her. No, she went a little mad. She scratched marks on the wall with her nails. She saw things. She seethed. Vengeance consumed her. She plotted ways to make Paul suffer. She devised ways to leave.

She hated Paul.

She truly hated him.

During the week of her isolation, Mark brought her meals. He also brought her Danae to breastfeed. He didn't speak to her. He simply lingered in the doorway watching her eat and observing her tend to the baby. Then he took Danae and left.

If Nyla ever thought Mark might be on her side regarding anything, she now knew differently.

When the week expired, Paul opened the door. "I made a trip into town for grains and beans. I hope you're happy."

Nyla didn't respond.

"I want you to make everyone spaghetti. If all plates aren't cleared, *you* will be put back in here."

With that, he turned around and walked away. Nyla stepped from the isolation room.

She went to the kitchen. She made a giant pot of spaghetti. She served it. Quietly, everyone ate—even Ava.

Later Nyla stood in the greenhouse staring at the poison garden. Something felt different about it. Like someone poked around in the dirt or took clippings. It worried her. It reminded her of Beatrice. Something seemed off then as well. Not long after, she used the garden to kill Carrie.

That thought nudged in, circling Nyla's brain. If Beatrice could use the poison garden on Carrie, why couldn't Nyla use it on Paul?

Not that she wanted to kill him. But why not make him unconscious? Then she, Ava, and the children would get the hell out of here, and—

"Hi," a quiet voice came from behind her.

Nyla turned to see Ava standing just inside the door. She wore a long blue cotton skirt. Darkness surrounded the greenhouse. Ava looked down. Nyla followed her gaze to the blood gathered around her ankles.

She rushed over.

Wincing, Ava clutched her arms. She bit back a cry of pain.

Nyla didn't know what Ava had eaten from the poison garden but it worked. She gave herself an abortion.

———

UPON DELIVERING the news of Ava's "miscarriage," Paul recoiled from her. He moved her into the room where

Sarah and Little Carrie slept. Nyla welcomed the news. She expected Ava to as well, but Ava seemed indifferent. She'd taken on a blank look that, as the next few months rolled by, never got better.

New rules appeared:

- Women are not allowed to talk to each other
- Women are not allowed to drink wine

Paul thought if Nyla and Ava talked, then they could plot ways to leave. He thought if they drank wine, it would make them inefficient homemakers.

Per the rules, Nyla forced herself to have sex with Mark. Then she would drink a special tea, the recipe of which she copied from *The Good and Bad Side of Herbs*. So far, no second pregnancy came. When Mark asked her why no second baby, she played stupid.

Paul went to town regularly. He never took Mark with him. No, Mark kept an eye on Nyla and Ava, making sure they followed the rules.

Paul also never brought anything back from town. Until a summer day when he did—a sixteen-year-old girl named Clementine, who was very pregnant with his baby.

Oddly enough she looked like June with small eyes and lips that didn't close over her teeth. She also wore a stupid smile. She was proud to be carrying Paul's baby. Proud to be sharing a mattress with him. Proud to have his attention.

Proud to be the only female allowed to have hair.

Proud to have loud sex every night.

Proud to be waited on by Ava.

Proud to be full-figured.

Because all of those things became rules as well:

- Anyone pregnant must not exert energy
- Anyone pregnant must not cut her hair
- Anyone pregnant must eat double the daily ratio
- All intimacy should be uninhibited

The rules made no sense. They became more ridiculous with each new one that appeared. They contradicted former rules.

On an overcast fall morning, Clementine went into labor. Fifteen hours later she screamed her head off as she gave birth to a healthy baby boy. Eight weeks later she announced a second pregnancy.

---

WINTER ARRIVED. Nyla turned twenty-two. Ava sank further into herself.

Clementine ruled the home.

One evening after sex with Mark, Nyla tiptoed downstairs to make her tea. She let it steep for ten minutes and drank the whole cup quickly. As she quietly washed the mug, a shadow shifted from behind her. Nyla looked up, seeing Clementine's reflection in the window above the sink.

The girl hiked her chin. "What did you just drink?"

"We're not allowed to be talking."

Clementine smirked. "You didn't see the new rule? *I'm* allowed to speak to you. I'm speaking now. What were you drinking?"

"Tea."

"What kind of tea?"

"Mint."

"Hm." Her lips puckered. "You drink that tea every time you and Mark have sex. You had sex tonight. I heard you. I think there's something in that tea."

Nyla made no expression. "It's mint, that's it." She left the kitchen. She went upstairs. She slid onto the mattress beside Mark. She watched Clementine come up the stairs and go into the room she shared with Paul.

Nyla's heart picked up pace. She stared at their doorway, waiting, waiting, waiting... but nothing happened.

Until the next morning.

She woke to find both Paul and Mark standing over her. Mark held her tin of tea. Paul presented a box full of plants he'd yanked from her poison garden. Clementine stood behind them, one hand on her pregnant belly and the other on her hip, smirking.

Nyla's heart pounded. She sat up on the mattress. She reached for Danae before remembering her daughter slept in the children's room now with Ava.

Paul said, "It has been brought to our attention that you are getting rid of life."

Nyla barely breathed.

Paul nodded to the box he held. "Your little poison garden is going away."

"You said you liked having something so deadly nearby," she reminded him, speaking out of turn and not caring.

He ignored her, nodding to the tin of tea. "As is this. How could you snuff out a baby? You disgust me."

A flame of fury built inside of her. She didn't care if she disgusted him. She hated him. "Yeah, well you disgust me. Look around. You're holding us in a prison." She shot straight up. "Look at *me*. Do you even recognize me? I am your daughter!"

Her explosion would lead to the isolation room. She

already knew this. She threw her hands up. "Might as well lead the way. I know where you're putting me."

# TWENTY-THREE

## LEAH

*Present Day*

IT'S BEEN hours since Nyla talked.

I listened, barely breathing, my heart racing, and my brain froze. I was in shock, yes, but also angry.

My daughter has been living in a commune for the past five years where she was told what to eat, made to sleep on a mattress, and forced to live without any doors. All while Paul and some man named Mark set ridiculous expectations and insane rules.

But that's not the way Nyla sees it.

She seemed—and still appears to be—enamored with the lifestyle. *We existed off the land,* she'd said. *We shared everything. We had no secrets. If done correctly, it's a great way to exist.*

*Where was this place?* I'd asked. *How many people were there? Why is your head shaved? Where is your baby?*

I had so many questions after she got done talking, but she answered none.

She slid from the island stool, grabbed a breakfast bar from the pantry, and told me she was going to go for a walk.

I let her go, but my God I needed to know so much more.

---

NYLA SPENDS a good portion of the day keeping to herself. She tinkers in her garden. She takes the rowboat down the river and back. She falls asleep in the swing on the back porch.

I spend most of the day researching communes and taking notes.

1. A group of people living together and sharing possessions
2. People join communes to share ideas and practice alternative ways of living
3. It attracts people who have been shunned by family and friends
4. Commune life offers little to no privacy and autonomy
5. This type of living centers around a small social circle
6. Often thought of as utopia living
7. Some turn into dangerous cults

The word cult strobes through my brain. I move on to researching that.

1. Misplaced admiration for a particular person
2. A small group regarded by others as having a strange or sinister way of living

3. People join cults attempting to gain independence and worth
4. Utilizes psychological manipulation and pressure strategies
5. Male members often sexually exploit female members
6. Cults live in isolation
7. Members are highly committed to a core set of beliefs

*Sinister. Manipulation. Sexually exploit. Isolation. Highly committed. Dangerous. Shunned by family.*

My gaze touches these words over and over again. Did I cause this? Did I shun Nyla and not even realize it?

I feel sick.

I stand up and pace away from the laptop. I walk over to the window and check on my daughter, finding her still asleep on the back porch swing cuddled under a blanket. With the sun setting soon, the temperature will drop. I don't want her to stay out much longer. Plus, she's barely eaten today.

I'm about to turn away when something in the distance catches my eye. Through the trees about fifty yards away, a blue truck sits parked on the mountain road.

That's the truck Nyla mentioned.

I turn away from the window, walk across the house, and straight out the front door. I charge down our driveway. Anger builds in me as I go. At the end of our road, I go left. The truck sits just up ahead. I can't see who is behind the wheel, but someone is.

"Hey!" I yell.

The truck's engine cranks. It pulls away.

I stand where I am, watching it go on up the mountain.

I don't move. I want whoever is driving to know I'm not intimidated.

When it disappears, I retrace my steps. Back in the house, I march upstairs. In the rear of the master closet is my father's old rifle. I've only shot this thing once. I doubt I remember how. Still, I grab the soft case and turn around.

I scream.

Nyla stands in the master suite, staring at me.

My hand slams over my heart. "Sorry."

She looks at the case. "What's going on?"

"I saw that blue truck."

Her face pales. "What? Where?"

"Out on the road that leads up the mountain."

She looks at the case. "Is that a rifle?"

"Yes." I walk out of the closet.

"What did you do?" she nervously asks.

I put the case on the bed and unzip it. "I charged after it. I yelled. It drove off." I look at her. "Who was driving that truck?"

"I don't know."

"Is that the truth or a lie?"

"The truth."

"But you know that truck."

"Yes."

"It's someone from the commune?"

She nods. "It could be one of two people."

"What do they want?"

"Me."

"Why?"

Her lips press together. She shakes her head.

I pick up the rifle. "I'm not sure I remember how to use this."

Nyla takes it from my hand. "Oh, I do."

# TWENTY-FOUR

## NYLA

*One Year Earlier*

THE OUTSIDE WORLD had no idea what went on—that women and children were being held against their will. If someone would have presented this scenario to Nyla four years ago when she first arrived, she'd have laughed and rolled her eyes.

Fast forward and she imagined the question: *Why not just leave?*

The answer came as a simple, *How?* How could Nyla and Ava, along with Sarah, Little Carrie, and Danae leave? They had access to a truck, but Paul kept the key on him at all times. The farm sat isolated, miles from civilization. The women and children wouldn't get far before the men found them.

Plus, Clementine constantly watched them.

The door to the isolation room opened. Clementine appeared. The first time Nyla had been locked up, it sufficiently beat her down. The second time, madness crept in. This time, Nyla welcomed the fury. She directed it at Paul.

She wanted him dead.

Clementine sniffed, taking a long second to let her eyes roam around the small room with its single mattress, sink, and toilet.

"What do you want?" Nyla demanded.

"You better be nice to me." She put a hand on her slightly swollen, pregnant belly. "I convinced Paul to let you have daily laps around the yard and visitation with Danae. Once you atone for what you did to Mark, Paul's agreed to let you out."

"By atoning you mean?"

"Pregnancy." She smirked. "Mark's agreed as well. He doesn't want to force you, though. He's not that kind of man. You need to apologize and *willingly* accept him into your bed. It's the least you owe him after ridding yourself of God knows how many fetuses."

"Fine."

Surprise flicked across her eyes.

Really, though, what choice did Nyla have? She needed out of this room. If getting pregnant by Mark did that, then so be it. "Send him in whenever."

---

LUCKILY, and like last time, Nyla instantly turned up pregnant.

Four weeks into her isolation, Paul opened the door. "Congratulations on being pregnant. Now go revive the garden. We need food." Then he walked away.

Clementine followed her to the greenhouse. She sat on a stool and monitored Nyla's every move. Nyla concentrated on weeding, fertilizing, planting, watering, and reviving her hard work.

Hidden in the blueberries, she tended to the one poison she'd kept.

Belladonna.

———

NYLA STAYED on her best behavior. She didn't speak unless spoken to. She tended her chores.

All the while, she plotted her escape.

She tried to share that plan with Ava countless times, but somehow Clementine always showed up as Nyla opened her mouth to speak.

For a teenage girl, Clementine proved to be a master of manipulation. She properly seduced Paul, wormed her way inside of his head, and somehow ran the place now. All while letting Paul think that he did.

Every few days, a new rule appeared, some specific only to Nyla:

- Even though Nyla is pregnant, she must still shave her hair
- Even though Nyla is pregnant, she's only allowed to gain fifteen pounds

Clementine had it in for her, and Nyla did not care. Clementine would not break her.

Eventually, Clementine realized this and turned her cruel energy on Ava. Clementine's words came vicious and picking. *You look horrible. Paul said you used to be a great beauty. What happened?*

Ava's already fragile existence shattered. Nyla truly feared she would take her own life.

Every chance available, she sent Ava an encouraging look or lovingly touched her. Ava never responded. She walked around in a perpetual state of silent submission. Nyla would give anything for Ava to grin again.

In late summer, Clementine once again screamed her head off as she gave birth to her second child. Paul preened.

Nyla's second baby came one morning in November. Like with Danae, everyone crowded in the bathroom to see the birth. Nyla looked Clementine firmly in the eyes as she pushed her second baby girl out. She didn't scream once.

# TWENTY-FIVE
## LEAH

*Present Day*

I WATCH in amazement as my daughter expertly handles my father's old rifle. She cleans it. She loads it. She demonstrates the proper way to hold it and fire it.

Other than Bill and Edna across the river, our next nearest neighbor lives about a half mile up the mountain. The sound of guns going off is a common thing around here. I don't hesitate in following Nyla outside to practice shooting.

She's remarkably good.

We practice for about an hour. Night finally settles in. Back inside the house, we engage the alarm. In the kitchen, I lay out vegetables and tempeh to roast. Quietly, Nyla chops fresh beets. I wash baby carrots. She lines a baking dish with parchment paper. I select spices.

"Tomorrow you'll be here one full week. Crazy, huh?"

"Mm."

"You okay?" I ask. She's barely said a word since coming inside.

"Yes."

I select a small red onion and peel it. "I think it would be a good idea if we stop at the police station tomorrow."

She stops chopping beets. "I don't want to do that. Please do not do that."

I look at her.

She's quick to say, "I mean, what can they do? They'll just tell you to keep the alarm on. It's not like anyone has done anything. Plus, if I remember, isn't the station at the bottom of the mountain? It's secluded up here. I can't see them doing any kind of complimentary drive-by."

I study her earnest face, a thought creeping in.

*I'm pretty damn sure my daughter is running from the law.*

# TWENTY-SIX
# NYLA

*Seven Days Earlier*

NYLA'S twenty-third birthday came and went. Winter moved into spring. Nyla patiently waited. Every day she recited a mantra:

> *Half rations*
> *Isolation room*
> *Rules*
> *Suggestion*
> *Karly*
> *Carrie*
> *Ava's rape*

Eventually, her plan would work.

You see, the thing about communal living—everyone helped themselves from the same platters. It made poisoning difficult. But, you see, the thing about Clementine—she loved being the exception to the rules. So, while Ava and Nyla were forbidden to drink wine, Clementine could.

Every night she, Paul, and Mark sat around the fireplace talking and sharing homemade wine made from grapes taken straight from Nyla's garden vines, specially grown in a fertile mix of belladonna and black earth.

In truth, Nyla didn't know when it would happen. Eventually, it would though, and she'd be ready.

On one sunny morning, Nyla woke. She breastfed Evie, her second child, now five months old. She went downstairs. Silently, she and Ava prepared breakfast.

Clementine woke up sick. She begged Nyla to make her some ginger tea. Nyla did.

Later in the morning, Mark came down ill as well. Nyla made him tea too.

Not long after that Paul followed.

Nyla moved all the children and Ava downstairs to the common room, making a show of "keeping them away from the germs."

"Nyla?" Paul croaked.

She raced into his room. "Yes?"

Weakly, he motioned her over. She knelt beside the mattress. His hand came up to her shoulder. "Make me some of that ginger tea, okay?"

Down in the common room, Ava rocked Clementine's youngest. Danae and her baby sister took a nap on a blanket. Little Carrie, Sarah, and Clementine's oldest colored in an old book.

Nyla came down beside Ava. She gripped her hand. "We're getting out of here," she whispered.

Ava frowned. "What are you talking about?"

"Just be ready." Nyla squeezed her fingers. "Get what we need for the children. I'll get the key to the truck and grab what cash I can find."

In the kitchen, she prepared ginger tea. Into three cups, she mixed more belladonna. Back upstairs she made sure Paul, Mark, and Clementine drank their tea.

Then she hovered in the shadows, waiting...

It only took five minutes to put the three of them into a deep sleep. Nyla worked quickly, getting the truck key from Paul, finding what cash she could, and helping Ava bundle the children into the truck.

"How long will they be out?" Ava nervously asked.

"A few hours," she lied. In truth, she didn't know.

"We can't take Clementine's children."

"Well, we can't leave them here either." Nyla's hand felt steadier than expected as she fit the key into the crank. She turned it. The truck didn't start. She turned it again. Again, it didn't start. She pressed the gas. She tried again.

On the passenger side, Ava held both of Clementine's children. Beside her, Little Carrie held Nyla's second baby, Evie. Next to Nyla sat Sarah with Danae on her lap. Six children in all—four under the age of three and all so very silent.

Nyla looked into Ava's wide, scared eyes. "I'm going to run for help."

"*What*? You can't leave me here. You can't leave us here."

Nyla reached across the children. She cupped Ava's face. "I know you're scared. I'm right there with you. Little Carrie will help."

The seven-year-old girl nodded.

"I'll run fast. I'll find someone to help us. I promise."

Then Nyla opened the driver's door. She paused. "Do you remember me telling you about my grandmother's cabin in Georgia?"

Ava nodded.

On the dash lay an old blue ballpoint pen. Nyla uncapped it. She found a scrap piece of paper under the driver's seat. She scribbled her grandmother's address. She handed the paper to Ava along with the cash she'd found. "If we get separated, meet me there."

Then, Nyla ran.

---

IT HAD BEEN five and a half years since Nyla first arrived at the farm. At the end of the long driveway, she paused. She didn't remember which way to go for town or the nearest neighbor.

She went right.

Dressed only in black leggings, old sneakers, and a long sleeve tee, she ran. And ran. And ran. Adrenaline and unadulterated fear propelled her forward.

What if she couldn't find anybody to help?

For thirty straight minutes, she ran. Her heart pumped. Her lungs screamed. One vehicle passed her, ignoring her frantic waves. She found two houses—one abandoned and one with no one home.

Her pace slowed. She gasped for breath. She screamed, "Someone help me!"

But no one answered.

She stood in the center of the road, dripping with sweat, looking ahead at the miles of deserted land.

A clear memory came of arriving to the farm all those

years ago. Ava drove. Nyla rode on the passenger side. They came from the other direction.

*No. No. No!*

Nyla took off, retracing her steps. She ran fast. Everything hurt—her feet, her legs, her heart, her lungs. She ignored it all.

Thirty minutes later, she approached the dirt driveway again. She stopped. Her chest heaved. She looked down the road. She didn't know how far help would be. She made a split decision to run back toward Ava and the truck. Maybe Nyla flooded it. Maybe it would start now.

She rounded the curve in the dirt driveway. The decrepit house came into view. Nyla's feet halted. She stared at the spot where the truck should be. The front door to the house stood open.

Breathing heavily, she slowly approached.

The ax Mark used to chop wood sat propped against the side of the house. She wrapped her hands around the hilt, squeezed tight, and brought it up, ready.

She stepped up onto the porch. Quietly, she listened. No sound came.

She moved through the open door. She shifted into the common room before going through the eating area and into the kitchen. She looked out the window, finding the barn and the greenhouse empty.

Her grip on the ax tightened even more.

One by one, Nyla moved up the creaky steps. As she neared the top, her feet froze in place. There on the landing lay Mark and Clementine, covered in vomit, eyes fixed wide, skin flushed red, not breathing.

*Guess the belladonna worked a little too well.*

Nyla stepped over them, moving toward Paul's room.

She took one step in, the ax up, her eyes darting to the mattress.

But Paul was nowhere to be found.

Neither was Ava.

# TWENTY-SEVEN
## LEAH

*Present Day*

NEITHER OF US speaks during dinner. We both pick at our food. We barely look at each other.

I take a sip of wine, eyeing her reflection in the dark windows.

Nyla glances up. Our eyes meet.

She says, "Fear is a powerful human emotion. It creates awareness. When you're scared, it forces you into your current moment. It makes you truly present. That's what you're feeling—fear. Allow it in. Accept it. Feel it."

"Stop it," I snap. "You sound like you're reciting someone else's words."

Something hits the window we're sitting in front of. I jump. Nyla lunges to her feet. She races across the kitchen to where we left the rifle. Outside, the motion detector lights flash on. A person dashes across the backyard.

I scream.

Nyla sprints over to the back door. She flings it open, charging out onto the porch.

"What are you doing?" I yell, racing after her.

I'm already dialing 911 when I step outside. *What the...*

Wearing a long burgundy corduroy dress with a white sweater, a young woman steps from behind a tree and into the light. Like my daughter, she also has a shaved head and looks extremely malnourished.

Nyla sucks in a breath.

She puts the rifle down and races from the porch across the yard. The two collide.

They stand, hugging. The young woman says, "I'm sorry it took me so long. I wasn't even sure this was the place."

Nyla grips her tighter.

I watch them, confused. Over the speaker, I hear, "Nine-one-one. What is your emergency?"

Nyla lets go of her friend and whips around to look at me. She shakes her head, mouthing *No. Please. Hang up.*

Her friend's eyes widen. She backs away. Nyla reaches for her.

My hand shakes.

"Nine-one-one. What is your emergency?"

Quickly, I take it off the speaker. "I'm sorry. I thought I had an intruder. Everything is okay."

While the emergency operator confirms, I watch Nyla and her friend hug again.

Eventually, I hang up.

The friend says, "I didn't mean to scare you just now."

"It's okay." Nyla lets go. "I was so worried Paul got to you. Is everyone okay?"

Her friend nods. "I got the truck started. I looked everywhere for you."

"I know you did."

"I've been driving up and down this mountain trying to figure out which house was yours." Her friend looks at me. "I'm sorry about earlier when you chased the truck. As I said, I wasn't sure."

Nodding, I pick up the rifle.

"Where's Paul?" Nyla asks.

"I don't know."

I look around the backyard, feeling uneasy. I walk the length of the porch, peering around the side of the house. In the distance, I can just make out the blue truck through the dark trees parked on the mountain road. I turn back around, now seeing Nyla and the young woman quietly talking.

Nyla looks up at me. "We'll be right back."

The motion detector lights blaze brightly, tracking their movement as they walk across the backyard, around the house, and down the driveway. They cut off and I barely make them out as they approach the truck. The dome light comes on as the friend gets behind the wheel and Nyla slides into the passenger side.

The dome light goes off.

The truck cranks. It backs up and turns around. It climbs my driveway.

I backtrack, going through the house and out the front door to meet them.

The truck parks. Both doors open. Nyla climbs out. She reaches back in to get something and emerges with a baby in her arms. Her friend does the same thing. As they step away, four other children file out, all underweight and the two oldest with buzzed cut hair.

I stare.

Nyla shuts the door. She leads the way across our front yard. I stay standing where I am on the front steps.

She stops in front of me. "Leah, this is Ava and these are our children."

# TWENTY-EIGHT

## THREE YEARS LATER

*Leah*

I sit on my back porch beside Walker, sipping iced tea and watching the kids play tag on this warm summer day. There's Carrie, now ten; Sarah, eight; Danae, five; and Evie, now three. On the other side of our property where the trail used to be, we built a second house for Nyla, Ava, and the children.

With the help of a friend of mine, we found a couple who adopted Clementine's kids.

Holding hands, Nyla and Ava step from their home. My daughter now rocks a cute pixie cut and Ava wears her hair in a short braid. Together, they walk past Nyla's greenhouse and over onto our yard to stand in the shade of an oak tree, smiling and watching the game of tag.

We've all been going to weekly counseling sessions where I've slowly come to hear the details of their life living with Paul and the other people. The farm in Middle

Tennessee where they lived for so many years was auctioned off. We told the authorities that Paul was responsible for Mark and Clementine's deaths.

In a way, he was.

Nyla and Ava live a quiet and secluded life. They make a living gardening and selling at our local farmer's market. Ava also sings and plays guitar at a coffee shop. They homeschool the children.

I won't go so far as to say my daughter and I have a perfect, loving relationship. But we understand each other and have mended fences.

Paul has never been found. We assume he stumbled from that horrible home and disappeared into the trees. Maybe he died in the surrounding woods. Maybe he found his way out. Who knows?

My gut tells me we'll never see him again.

---

### Nyla

NYLA REFUSED to listen to fear. It was the one "gift" from her years with her father. He had it all wrong. Fear could be transposed into strength. She no longer lived under his ideology. She lived for herself, Ava, and the children.

Over the past three years they had developed their own set of rules:

- Eat whenever you are hungry
- Laugh and talk as much as you would like

- Celebrate all birthdays and holidays with joy
- Feel your emotions
- Dance
- Play
- Love who you want to love

If Paul ever dared to reappear, Nyla knew where her grandfather's rifle was kept. And she was an excellent shot.

# EPILOGUE

## TEN YEARS LATER

### Mass Suicide Linked to Cult

---

*Following an anonymous tip, police entered a farm house in rural Kentucky and discovered nine victims of a mass suicide.*

*The deceased—five women and three men of varying ages—were all found lying in one room. It was later revealed that the men and women were members of a cult, whose leader proclaimed that suicide was the ultimate show of no fear and trust in a greater way to exist.*

*The cult was led by Paul Peters, a sixty-five-year-old man, who had come to live on the farm eight years earlier. He persuaded others to abandon their families and possessions and move to rural Kentucky where he promised a better and simpler way of life. Peters and his followers drank a lethal mixture of Belladonna and wine and then lay down to die.*

*Three children were found unharmed and locked in a room. They are currently in custody while officials try to locate the immediate families.*

# BOOKS BY S. E. GREEN

### The Lady Next Door

How well do you know your neighbor?

### Killers Among

Lane swore never to be like her late mother. But now she too is a serial killer.

### Monster

When the police need to crawl inside the mind of a monster, they call Caroline.

### The Third Son

All he wants is a loving family to belong to, to manipulate, to control...

### Vanquished

A secret island. A sadistic society. And the woman who defies all odds to bring it down.

### Mother May I

Meet Nora: Flawless. Enigmatic. Conniving. Ruthless.

# ABOUT THE AUTHOR

S. E. Green is the award-winning, best-selling author of young adult and adult fiction. She grew up in Tennessee where she dreaded all things reading and writing. She didn't read her first book for enjoyment until she was twenty-five. After that, she was hooked! When she's not writing, she loves traveling and hanging out with a rogue armadillo that frequents her coastal Florida home.

Made in the USA
Las Vegas, NV
28 May 2023

72633207R00090